ENCHANTED SOUL

Novel By
Sir Patrick Bijou

DESCRIPTION

Do You Want to Be Thrilled, Horrified, and Shocked to Your Core?

Immerse yourself in a thrilling horror story filled with skillfully crafted and mind-blowing twists that will thrill you, shock you and leave you with lingering feelings of uneasiness and dread.

London Art Gallery... Death of a woman... Event that will change Gabe's life forever...

Gabriel Herrison is a photographer that had come to look at the National Gallery paintings for inspiration. He was in need of ideas of ways to set his work apart. One thing he had not expected to see through his camera lens, however, was the young woman who had rushed in off the street and now stood transfixed in front of a painting.

Instinctively, feeling he was watching something that doesn't really happen every day, Gabe began to snap pictures of the scene with his camera.

It all happened so suddenly that many of those watching took a few moments to work out why she had said nothing. She gave a cough and it was blood bubbled up from her lips not words.

Sticking from the back of her neck was a long, feathered shaft. She had been shot with an arrow.

Enchanted by the event that unraveled in front of his eyes, Gabe gets drawn into a thrilling cat-and-mouse game trying to solve the poor girl's murder.

Unfortunately for him, it seems that some sinister and maybe even supernatural forces are trying to prevent him from learning the truth...

Will he be able to find the killer, or will he lose his head in the process?

ABOUT THE AUTHOR

Sir Patrick is an eclectic writer, lives in the United Kingdom and was born in 1958 in Georgetown and raised in London, England.

His diverse writing prowess has been influenced by many experiences.

He pursued several courses of study at several universities, and declared two majors during his schooling which included the areas of Business and Economics and finally obtained his doctorate in Economics and International banking.

In all these scholastic studies though, the true treasures he took away are not the certificates (though those are very important), but instead the experiences he had, the people he met, the foods he ate and even the places he stayed.

"In truth, I am a citizen of the world and this greatly influences my writing.

So, if you are already a fan of mine, I appreciate you. If you are not yet one, then what are you waiting for? Read a book and then read some more. I create characters that resonate with you and infuse life into all I write".

Finding my Books
Sir Patrick has written over 15 published fictional and non-fictional books across several genres, I have realized the need to make it easier for my readers to find my books.

I would appreciate if you would be kind enough to leave a review of this book.

TABLE OF CONTENTS

ENCHANTED SOUL PART 1

CHAPTER 1

The corridors and rooms of London's National Gallery are used to unusual sights. The Gallery is, after all, home to one of the finest collections of paintings from all around the world and, on any given day, visitors are likely to be greeted by thousands of unexpected moments within their ageing canvases. However, the sight that greeted tourists on this particular rainy Monday morning was an especially strange one as it did not exist in any of the myriad images displayed on the Gallery walls.

Martin Wilkins, the guard standing behind the tall classical style pillars of the Gallery's 19th Century portico, had spent the morning idly watching the pigeons in Trafalgar Square. His job rarely, if ever, involved any actual security and his mind liked to wander. However, this morning, he suddenly caught a flash of something moving very fast across the square, dashing towards the entrance of the Gallery.

As the figure approached the steps up to the Gallery entrance, Martin was able to discern that it was a middle-aged woman. She was dressed curiously for the weather in nothing but a thin white smock. Even stranger when crossing the dirty wet flagstones of the square, she was wearing nothing at all on her feet. She seemed to be in a great rush but every now and again threw a panicked look over her shoulder as if paranoid that she was being followed. Martin glanced in the direction of her frightened looks but could see nothing. He concluded the woman was probably suffering a mental episode.

Entrance to the Gallery was free these days so the strange woman would not be requiring a ticket. She wasn't exactly causing any trouble with her unusual dress and panicked hurry. After weighing up his options for a moment, Martin decided that perhaps he had better stay out of this, there was no cause to go challenging someone in her mental state, it would only cause more trouble than good. He would let the other Gallery staff inside deal with her.

Penny Scott had come to the Gallery every Monday for the past two years. She was gradually working her way through the collection. She was retired; her husband had passed on, leaving her to pursue her interest in art alone. Each week she would spend the whole day studying each painting she came across individually for sometimes hours at a time, peering into the tiniest little details of the paintwork.

On this particular Monday, Penny was distracted from her close up study of Peter Paul Rubens' Judgement of Paris by something of a commotion from the Gallery's other visitors. A hushed but judgemental whisper was running through the usually quite corridors and it was accompanied by a sight that Penny, with her hours of study of still images was almost two slow of eye to see properly. It looked to her, however, like a woman racing through the gallery in her bare feet, rain dripping from her body. She seemed to be heading with some purpose and little regard for others.

Penny simply tutted to herself, muttering under her breath about how a woman like that should be old enough to know better, and turned back to the baroque image of the prince pondering over the full figures of the three naked goddesses. She gave the woman's unusual behaviour no further thought until she saw a report on the ITN News later that evening.

Student Persephone Cross found herself in the National Gallery that morning almost by accident. Increasingly these days, she found that she had a lot of time to kill and decided that wandering amongst the works of the great masters would be a pleasant enough way to achieve this, especially if it got her out of the rain.

Like many others that day, she was more than a little surprised by the sight of a rain soaked, barely dressed woman running through the galleries.

Standing in the room of 17th Century Spanish works, Persephone got a good look at the woman as she ran in. There was an expression on her face of pure terror the like of which the student had never seen before and hoped never to see again. Persephone could see in the frightened woman's face the certainty that her time was almost up and she could do nothing about it. The thought sent a shiver down Persephone's spine as the other woman's hurried sprint stopped abruptly right beside her.

Even though her body had stopped dead still, her face was still animated in panic. Her breathing was deep and heavy after the effort of having run who knows how far. Persephone could see the woman's eyes darting about all over the place, flitting across different parts of the room, never settling anywhere for too long until they looked right into Persephone's. The student girl was now the one who didn't know where to look when faced with that stare of pure desperation. Curiosity mingled with fear in Persephone's breast as the terrified woman opened her mouth to speak.

Photographer Gabriel Herrison had come to look at the National Gallery paintings for inspiration. He was in need of ideas of ways to set his work apart. A friend, well, an acquaintance really, who was a rather more successful photographer, had told him that perhaps the greatest artists of previous centuries might be able to help him out and had recommended that a day at the National Gallery could bring all the inspiration he needed. One thing he had not expected to see through his camera lens, however, was the young woman who had rushed in off the street and now stood transfixed in front of a painting.

Diego Velazquez' Rokeby Venus is one of the best-loved paintings in the entire gallery and, even without the unusual presence of the bewildered and frightened woman, it would normally draw a bit of a crowd. Now, everybody in the room began to push closer, eager to find out just what was going on. Instinctively, feeling he was watching something that doesn't really happen every day, Gabe began to snap pictures of the scene with his camera.

Everyone waited with bated breath as the woman opened her mouth to speak. She seemed to be about to enunciate something but nothing came out but a gasp. It all happened so suddenly that many of those watching took a few moments to work out why she had said nothing. She gave a cough and it was blood bubbled up from her lips not words. Blood began to gush from her throat; there was an open wound there. As she dropped to her knees and slumped forward, the cause of the injury was obvious. Sticking from the back of her neck was a long, feathered shaft. She had been shot with an arrow.

Instantly, the watching people spun around looking for the archer but there was nobody else in the room. Gabe, continuing to watch from behind his camera viewfinder, still took photo after photo. Afterwards, he was convinced that he had seen a flash of white, like the material of someone's dress, fluttering rapidly away from the doorway but this did not show up in any of his photographs.

Turning back to the body slumped on the floor, Gabe could see a group of people already bent over her, feeling her pulse and pronouncing that there was no life in her. At the same time, he saw that she was not slumped on the floor where she had fallen. Her hand was stretched out in front of her, her fingers stained with the blood of her neck wound. On the wall beneath the famous painting, the dying woman had scrawled a picture or design in blood. It was a circle with a cross protruding beneath it and an arrow coming from the upper right hand side, at roughly the six and two positions if it were a clock face. Gabe didn't have the slightest idea what it could mean but, feeling it could be important, made sure surreptitiously to snap a photo of it.

That night, Gabe dreamt a dream that he had not had in about a decade, only things had changed in the dream in the intervening years even as they had changed in Gabe. He had spent all afternoon hanging around waiting in the police station before being briefly questioned about the morning's incident in a routine fashion and sent on his way. The events of the morning, however, continued to play on Gabe's mind.

It wasn't the image of the dead woman with panic in her eyes coughing up blood that had stuck in his mind so much as the painting she had died in front of. Gabe was no art expert but he knew what he liked and this was one painting that seemed to draw him right in. There was something in the composition that seemed to arouse his interest. The way that the woman's body had her back turned towards the viewer seemed far more tantalising and mysterious than other reclining nude images. Gabe was also fascinated by the figure's shapely body the way her soft white thighs curved towards her narrow hip. Seeing the enigmatic expression on the indistinct reflection on her face in the mirror brought Gabe's mind back to his childhood fantasies about Venus, the Queen and Mistress of Love.

When looking back on his dream on awaking the following morning, Gabe realised that it was no doubt informed by these preoccupations but, just for a moment in that deep and magical slumber, he felt like the world of ancient gods and goddesses could return to him like it had in his childhood.

With the image of the Velazquez painting playing through his mind as he dropped off, Gabe soon found himself transported to a land of bright blue cloudless skies and forests of trees and vines and white flowers. He was walking on grass as soft as velvet as a tinkling of running water could be heard from somewhere just out of sight. Gabe walked towards where the sound was coming from and arrived at a brook of crystal clear water. He walked towards the water's edge to discover he was not alone.

Lying on the bank of the stream was a woman, tall, slender and elegant. Gabe's heart skipped a beat the moment he saw her. Even with her back to him, he instantly knew her from the cascades of golden hair. She was admiring her reflection in the clear waters of the pool and Gabe could just about make out the shape of her face from the waters.

It was Venus herself, just like in his childhood dreams and, just like in his childhood dreams, he felt like he had lost all control of his own body on seeing her naked beauty. Something stirred within him, an overwhelming sensation of desire. The feelings of those childhood dreams began to make sense to him now. When he was so young, he could not properly understand how the sensuous Queen of Love would make people feel but now he did. All his body was alive with yearning and all of his blood seemed to rush faster than it ever had before, with his heart beating harder and harder to catch up. He felt himself become aroused and his penis stiffen, growing proud and hard against his will.

It was at this point that Gabe realised that he too was naked, like the paragon of beauty herself and he felt a flush of shame all run all over him just as fast as his arousal. He felt suddenly especially awkward in his skinny body and full of embarrassment about how he could have so little control over how it behaves. He felt himself suddenly very unattractive and sought for some way to hide his nakedness and his arousal but there was nothing to hide behind amongst the soft grass.

Just as Gabe began to panic, the reclining Venus appeared to notice his presence reflected in the water. She inclined her head a little towards him and spoke in that rich musical voice that Gabe had all but forgotten but that now brought back so many childhood memories and set his flesh tingling.

"Why do you feel ashamed?" she asked, "You are becoming beautiful."

Gabe blinked and then realised that he wasn't standing there watching, he was the one reclining by the river looking at the reflection in the water. The long necked goddess knelt beside him. She cupped her hands into the water and poured the cold, clear liquid from her hands onto Gabe's head. Gabe gasped as the cold water ran across his warm, lively skin.

"These waters will baptise you afresh," the lyrical voice seemed to come from right inside his head, "And you will be new born in beauty."

Her wet hands ran down his body and each tiny touch that her fingertips made against his naked skin felt incredible. He no longer felt any shame at all in his nakedness or the hardness of his arousal. All he wanted was to give his body up to pleasure. As he turned his attention back to the pool, he could see his reflection in the glass clear water. Only, it wasn't him at all. The figure that looked back at him was a beautiful woman with soft round breasts and a narrow waist.

Looking down at his own body, Gabe was disappointed to find the reflection was not accurate, he still had the same old pale and thin male body he had always had, only now with his manhood more erect and proud than it had been in a long time. The unimaginably gentle and tender touch of the golden haired goddess moved across Gabe's chest. He shivered and awoke.

He was no longer in the paradise of his dreams. The soft green grass and crystal clear water disappeared along with the sensual love goddess. It was just Gabe alone in bed in his dark, empty flat, with a rather embarrassing hard erection and morning beginning to stream through the window. He had to get up and think about work.

Gabe sat at his desk with his laptop open, staring blankly at the screen. His mind was still far away. He couldn't help thinking about the previous morning and now his thoughts were not all fantasies of love goddesses. His mind was just starting to process properly that he had seen a woman killed right in front of him.

For some reason, the fact that he had watched the whole incident through the viewfinder of his bulky camera made it easier to cope with. It was almost as if viewing things through the camera made it feel like they were happening a long way away to other people, like watching the images on the news. He had heard that this was how photographers were able to operate seeing traumatic things in war zones, by hiding behind the camera to document events then it would seem like they were never really there at all. That was how Gabe had been all his adult life, concealed and detached behind his camera while the world went on around him. He had realised that this was the best way to avoid any pain to his sometimes over sensitive spirit, and he had resigned himself perhaps to not being truly part of anything but always to observe from the sidelines.

He began to upload the pictures that he had taken at the National Gallery onto the computer and they flashed up on the screen, quickly cycling through the events of the day. Starting with shots of pleasant, calm landscapes, the photos quickly became a document of the bloody scene that was on all the news channels.

Now that they were on his screen, Gabe could not look away. He was hooked. He felt that he had to try and understand what he had seen. Looking with the detachment of seeing a photograph on a computer screen, he could take himself away from having actually been there and examine the murder as a puzzle to be solved. He had turned copies of the pictures over to the police but a part of his mind, the part that liked to absently daydream, wondered if he could solve this mystery first. Anyway, it would be a good way to take his mind off the sickening reality.

Now that frail feminine body stretched out on the floor, blood stained body barely covered by the white shift, became like the victim in a mystery show on TV rather than a traumatic personal memory. Gabe began to study the picture closely, the arrow stuck from the back of her neck and there was a pool of blood all around it. She had slumped awkwardly on the floor but this was not the pose the photo had caught her in. Her arm was outstretched and her hand stained dark red with the blood from her own neck wound. Something had compelled her to use her very last breath to write on the wall in her own blood.

Gabe switched to the next photo, a close up of the bloody symbol on the gallery wall. The simple shape seemed to have a certain familiarity to Gabe but he couldn't quite place where he might have seen it before. He knew he had seen a circle with a cross or an arrow like that, but he just couldn't place it. He knew it had to be important, however. He wondered if there was any connection between the symbol and where it had been drawn, whether the renaissance masterwork had any link to the shocking modern murder.

The young woman had seemed to rush with purpose. She seemed curiously out of place on a wet, grey London day, without shoes or many clothes. It was almost as if she was escaping from something and yet the National Gallery seems a strange place to go if you were trying to escape. She seemed to have headed there for a purpose, perhaps this particular painting had something to do with it. The arrow in her neck seemed a curious choice of weapon, belonging to a different age and, perhaps, with a symbolic significance of its own. The painting, the symbol, the arrow, all of them seemed parts of a puzzle that Gabe could not fit together.

He decided to change his focus. Staring at the symbol was getting him nowhere, there must be something else to consider, another clue that could be the key to revealing the secrets behind the other mysteries as if when that one thing was discovered everything else would just fall into place and the whole affair would seem so obvious that he would wonder why he hadn't thought of it in the first place.

He began to think about what else might have made that space in the gallery particularly unusual on that day. Maybe the painting had nothing to do with it. Naturally, he began to consider the possibility that the Rokeby Venus was not significant in and of itself, but could perhaps have been a meeting point. The dead woman could have had something that she desperately needed to say or to pass on before whatever it was that was chasing her caught up with her.

Scanning the crowd gathered round the body in his many photos, Gabe searched for anyone who seemed slightly out of place in a normal gallery visiting crowd. A rather doughy looking security guard bent over the body with an expression on his face that conveyed more frustration at this inconvenience than shock at the murder. Although that seemed a little callous, Gabe considered that the presence of the guard was certainly not unusual in the gallery.

An elderly woman, her milky white eyes glaring through thick glasses, looked on disapprovingly, at the gawping crowd that prevented her from getting to the painting, at the messy pool of blood and the symbol defacing the wall. She looked like she thought that the sudden and brutal murder was simply a sign of declining moral standards in the young. Gabe guessed there was nothing all that unusual in that either. None of these people seemed to view the corpse stretched out in agony on the floor with anything more than a dispassionate sneer. They couldn't have had any personal connection with the strange events.

Frustrated, Gabe cycled back through the earlier shots, the ones he had taken around the gallery before the murder. Suddenly, something caught his eye. A picture that he had taken of the room in which he just happened to catch the bare footed woman in her last living moments, standing exhausted, staring at the painting of the beautiful goddess lounging with her back to the rest of the room. It was not the victim, however, that Gabe's eyes were drawn to. No, it was another woman who he had not noticed from any of the other pictures.

That in itself would be enough to throw Gabe's suspicions on the mystery woman. She had been in the gallery before the murder had happened. She had witnessed it and then disappeared. Surely, Gabe reasoned, the natural thing to do when something like this had occurred would be to stick around and see what would result from it, at least see if the woman was indeed dead. However, Gabe's curiosity was really aroused by the fact that the mystery woman and the soon to be victim were looking right at each other as if the barefoot one had something she was desperate to say to the other.

Finally, the woman's very appearance marked her out as that unusual, out of place thing that Gabe had been scanning the other photos for, although Gabe didn't really know where this woman would be in her right place. Amidst the smart, grey, unremarkable art-appreciating crowd, this young woman stood out a mile. Gabe's eyes were instantly drawn to her hair, the brightest thing in the room. It was cut in a savage bob and died a bright purple colour that simply invited people's attention and, quite probably, their disapproval. Gabe could guess that this was a woman who took great pleasure in being quite confrontational, maybe even violent. Her face glinted with piercings, one in her lip, a stud in her nose and a row of them around her ear lobe.

She was wearing a very short black mini-skirt that barely extended below the array of studded belts and chains around her waist. Gabe knew that the skirt was designed to draw attention to her legs in torn fishnets but he couldn't help his eyes from travelling just there. With her small stature, her giant footwear looked slightly comical, a pair of huge black platform biker boots with a series of glinting buckles up the side. Looking at the combination of sexually provocative fishnets and tough, practical boots, left Gabe convinced that this was perhaps a rather confused young woman.

The whole effect of the outfit, hair and piercings was enough to make Gabe both a little scared and fascinated.

He tried to imagine what sort of woman would want to stand out so much. He pictured someone barely out of their teens, a little lost and alienated and ready to join in with any group or ideal that would have her, someone whose tendency towards aggressive, confrontational behaviour could be harnessed by someone older, wiser, more manipulative. Gabe knew that such a person could prove dangerous, could be mixed up in something pretty nasty.

Of course, these were just guesses but Gabe was the kind of guy who sometimes let his imagination run away with him. This wasn't the first time during his life as an aspiring photographer that he had tried to identify a whole personality and life story from a blurry image in one of his photos. Still, he became increasingly convinced that the young punk woman was the key to this mystery. Zooming in closer on the section of the photo that contained her image, Gabe became more and more convinced by this until he saw something that left him in no doubt.

The woman's arms and upper body were decorated with a variety of tattoos that became clearer as Gabe zoomed his image browser to focus on her and her alone. One very quickly caught his eye as it instantly reminded him of a design he had seen before, and not all that long ago. He could only see part of the design, the top half was obscured by the sleeve of her t-shirt, but that was enough for Gabe. The curve of the bottom half of a circle with a cross on the underside, hanging beneath the circle. He knew just where he had seen that before. It was the same as the symbol painted in blood on the gallery wall. Now Gabe knew there must be some connection between the two women.

He gasped a sharp intake of breath. It was one thing suspecting something, but it was quite another to be confronted with the evidence. His head felt light. Suddenly, there was a sense that he had grasped some thread with which he could unravel the whole confusing web. The mystery had completely sucked him in by now. He was totally absorbed in it so his mind could barely think of anything else.

Breathing heavily and excitably, he managed eventually to calm himself down. So, he had a clue, some evidence, what could he do with it? Once his initial thrill had gone, Gabe had to admit that the discovery led him no nearer to solving anything. The woman, despite how much Gabe might study the one blurred image he had of her, remained a complete mystery. Without her, he realised, he was still stuck at square one.

As the escalator descended deep into the earth, Gabe slumped his shoulders, lost in thought. There was a large crowd rushing to and fro about the business of the day through Leicester Square tube station, but Gabe seemed not to be a part of them, he did not seem to see them or to interact with them. He had just retreated inside himself and his own thoughts and the world just had to move around him.

On the platform, he waited for the train to pull up, staring at the advertising plastered on the wall on the other side of the tunnel, promising exciting new West End shows he had no interest in seeing. He wasn't really taking in what he could see on the posters, the image in his mind was still that of the goddess Venus, her back towards him, looking back at him curiously through a mirror, and of the frail body of a young woman in a pool of blood, stretched out before the goddess, drawing signs on the wall.

On the train, the regular rumble along the tracks served only to lull him further into his thoughts as he stared at the map above him, tracing the dark blue line through the various stops, wishing, imagining that there was a thread so easily marked out for him to follow now. If only this cryptic crime had handy lines of bright colour, he could follow to their termination rather than the tangled web of questions without answers, puzzles without solutions.

After his moment of triumph when he had seen the young woman with the purple hair in his photo and discovered her tattoo, Gabe had thought that he might be getting somewhere towards understanding, but now he realised that the whole thing was just as much of a mystery as ever. The only thing that had happened in the last day since this first discovery was that Gabe had become more and more obsessed. What had started out as a distraction for his troubled mind, something to take his thoughts away from the disturbingly sickening reality of the slumped corpse leaking blood, had turned his mind even more troubled. He felt that he couldn't let it go, he felt drawn on down the line, like the train he rode over whose direction he had no control, only in this he had no map either.

He had returned to the Gallery that afternoon in the hope that the painting or its surroundings could help with his thoughts. As much as anything, he just needed a change of scene from staring at his laptop screen, analysing every inch of his photos, looking for tiny details he might have missed, examining all of the people surrounding the body. Even at the Gallery, he had got the computer out and had compared his photos to the present state. The room had re-opened that day after the Metropolitan Police forensics team were done with it and now it looked as though nothing untoward had ever happened here. The bloodstains were clear from the floor and the symbol, mention of which Gabe had seen in none of the newspaper or TV reports of the murder, no longer defaced the wall. In fact, the whole trip had proved singularly useless in giving Gabe any new thoughts.

Now, as he travelled back to his small, dark flat to stew in his morbid thoughts, Gabe began to think that he should pull himself together. The police had all of the information that he did and were much better equipped to piece it together and to track down the appropriate witnesses. That was provided they had seen the purple haired punk who made a very quick exit from the murder scene.

As for Gabe, he couldn't take his mind off the woman. In fact, his mind simply seemed to cycle between images and visions of the three women; the unfortunate victim, her throat pierced and the blood pouring from her mouth, the goddess Venus, posing seductively, and the purple haired woman, frowning in confusion, frustration or anger. As his eyes passed across his fellow passengers on board the rattling underground train, he began to see these three everywhere, in the faces of all the women around him.

Looking through the window in the door that separated his carriage from the next, Gabe could see a lurid shock of purple hair standing out amidst the commuter crowd. He knew that it wasn't completely unique for a woman to colour her hair that shade but even so he began to see the woman from the Gallery, the woman from his photo. He couldn't help himself. He stared into the next carriage, trying to get a real look at the woman, to see whether his mind was once more imbuing a random traveller with the face of the woman he had become obsessed with or whether it was really her.

As the train came rushing into the station, she turned her head and Gabe caught a glimpse of piercings, one in the lip, a stud in the nose and a row in the ear lobe. It had to be her. As she stepped onto the platform Gabe, without thinking, hurried off the train, following her. He had no idea what he was doing, what he wanted to see, whether he wanted to confront her and what he would say when he did, still he found himself tailing her path out of the station and up onto the street.

Fortunately, she was easy to follow and Gabe was able to stay back at some distance and still keep a good eye on her. Although she wasn't all that tall, that purple hair could be picked out in any crowd and they were far enough from the real busiest parts of the city for there not to be too big crowds. Gabe spent enough of his life on the outside of whatever was happening, observing but not getting in the way, as was the photographer's role, that stalking actually proved surprisingly easy. Although maybe stalking would not have been the word he would have used to himself.

They were in Islington and it was the middle of the afternoon and, as they headed away from the tube station, the streets became quieter and quieter and Gabe began to worry that the purple haired woman would notice that he was following behind her and the confrontation he was unsure about would be forced upon him. She didn't look big but she did look like she could take him on. Gabe had never been particularly strong and certainly hadn't the slightest clue how to handle himself in a fight. He had never been in one and the idea made him feel slightly sick.

She cut across a park and Gabe followed. They were now alone on the path, cut off from the relatively busy area of the street by a high fence and trees. Suddenly everything seemed much quieter. Gabe began to walk with a lot more care, staying significantly further back from the woman he was watching. At one point, he even dropped to the floor and pretended to be having a serious problem with his shoelaces when he saw the woman turn back as if startled by having heard something behind her.

After a moment, she turned back to the path and continued on her way. Gabe stayed on his knees for a second to watch and in that moment discovered that they were not as alone as he had previously felt. It wasn't his movement that had startled the woman. Two figures were quietly making their way through the trees, moving towards the path. Their movement was almost imperceptible, barely making a rustle in the tree line, but Gabe was used to watching, to observing and paying very close attention and he saw it. He saw that they were closing in on her pretty fast. His heart began to pound and there was a lump in his throat, what should he do? Turn and run, rush to help the woman, or take this as an opportunity to catch and question her.

He didn't have a moment more to think about it as two male figures came springing from the tree line to grab the woman. Both were unnaturally tall, at least 6 foot 5, probably a lot more, with an oddly wiry shape and long arms. They both had pale, shaved heads with heavy, frowning brows. They were dressed identically in what might be a long coat or cape, beneath which could be anything for all Gabe could see.

She kicked one of them in the shin with her big heavy biker boots and her elbow flew back to connect with the second right in the chest. She turned to run but they recovered quickly. As they grabbed her arms, she continued to thrash and kick but they silenced her by pulling out long knives. As all this happened, all Gabe did was watch and now he heard one of the men lean in to her and speak. His voice was a high-pitched lisping hiss but the sound of it carried all the way to Gabe.

"From now on, the rest of your life will be a living nightmare, for we are fear and we are dread!"

In a second, Gabe was up on his feet and running. He still didn't have clue what he was doing or why, he was acting on pure instinct. He knew that he could not just wait and watch this woman be attacked and do nothing, even if he did think she might be dangerous herself, even if the very situation he now observed suggested she was indeed mixed up in something nasty. Or maybe that was just the reason, maybe a part of him felt that with this assault, these mystery attackers were taking away his best chance of understanding what had happened at the National Gallery a few days earlier.

Whatever the reason, he saw the young woman in the grip of one of the sinister tall men as the other brandished a knife, really more of a ceremonial dagger, towards her. The woman had an expression on her face that mixed defiance with fear but for the moment, the knife had kept her still.

Gabe kept running until he caught up with the three figures. Getting closer, he realised that the two men were even taller than he had previously thought, their bodies slightly contorted and hunchbacked. Their eyes displayed a blank, dark expression completely lacking in any human compassion. Gabe knew that whatever the woman had done, he could not leave her to men such as these.

He still didn't know what to do but he had the advantage of surprise. The two men had all their attention, all their hate, focused on one spot, the young woman before them. Gabe knew he wasn't strong, he wasn't violent, but he was fast. His only hope was to use his surprise advantage and get away before they realised what hit them. All of these calculations flew through his mind in a few seconds until he was literally right on top of the group.

Pure instinct kept a hold over him and he found himself swinging his shoulder bag, in which he carried his heavy laptop, through the air. It connected with the knife wielding man on his temple with a sickening crunch, knocking him to the floor. The second man, shocked at the assailant appearing as if from nowhere, loosened his grip on the woman's shoulders.

She appeared as surprised as they were at Gabe appearing from nowhere, but fortunately was quick to seize her advantage. The man standing over her was a good head taller than she was, which just happened to be the perfect height for her head to swing back and connect hard with his chin, sending him reeling back from her. She swung back towards him and landed a hard kick straight between his legs, sending her biker boots heavily into his groin. He winced but nothing more, as if the pain was just a slight twinge.

With the second man still floored for the moment, Gabe swung his laptop bag again and hit the first on the back of his head causing him to stagger and lose his focus. The young woman grabbed Gabe's arm and pulled him away.

"Run!" she yelled, as the two men picked themselves up and turned, faces black with rage, towards Gabe and his new companion.

Gabe didn't need any more encouragement than that and, in a second, he had turned tail and made a dash for the gates of the park, taking them out onto the street. The purple haired woman had a start on him but soon Gabe had caught her up and their heavy footfalls and panting breaths fell in unison, Gabe's heavy bag bouncing painfully against his side. With each step, their two pursuers, with much greater strides, caught up that little bit further.

They skidded through the gates and out onto the main road, it was mostly deserted, there was no help for them here. Continuing to run as fast as his legs could carry him, Gabe glanced over his shoulder to see the two men turn out of the park gates just a few yards behind them. Very soon, they would be caught once more and Gabe did not want to find out what these knife-wielding maniacs would be like to people who had escaped their clutches once.

They raced towards the next road and, not looking to see if there was any passing traffic, ran straight out across it. Gabe, who was slightly in front, ran straight into the front of a large black car that was just about to pull out, sending him reeling back into the woman's arms. She pushed him forward off her and then grabbed his arm with one hand and opened the car door with the other. Gabe just had time to notice it was a taxi cab and it was empty.

"Get in," said the purple haired woman, in a pronounced, precise, cut glass accent that Gabe had certainly not expected to come from her.

He did not, however, have time to ponder this as they bundled inside the back of the cab and slammed the door behind them, locking it just as their two pursuers reached the road. They glared through the window at Gabe and his companion with ill-disguised hate and anger.

"Drive," said the woman to the cab driver in the commanding tones usually associated with the mistress of the house addressing a servant.

"Where to, love?" he responded.

"Anywhere but here."

Gabe let out an audible sigh of relief as the taxi pulled away and left the two tall, angry men standing by the roadside far behind. It was only then that he was able to collect his thoughts and turn to his companion on the back seat. He suddenly realised that he was now basically alone with the woman he had considered dangerous and potentially violent. He had told nobody what he was doing. He could just disappear completely and nobody would know. Still, at least now was a chance to confront her, to understand finally what on earth was going on here. He opened his mouth to speak but she got in first.

"So," she turned to him, an edge of aggression in those precise, educated tones, "Who the hell are you? And why the fuck are you following me?"

The swearword sounded odd, out of place in her well- educated accent, giving it perhaps an extra edge. Gabe was shocked. He opened his mouth to speak but couldn't figure out what on earth to say. It wasn't important anyway, as she seemed quite happy to carry on.

"I mean, don't get me wrong, I'm grateful for you helping me out of that sticky situation back there, but I don't take kindly to being stalked. I can take care of myself pretty well, especially from the likes of you, pretty boy," she glared at him, a challenge obvious in her voice.

"I think you're the one who owes me an explanation," Gabe shot back, given courage by her aggressive delivery, "I've just saved your life, the least you could do is tell me who those guys were and what this is all about?"

"Me? How the fuck should I know?" she said, seeming genuinely surprised that he would expect her to be aware of the situation, "They just came out of fucking nowhere. I'm just minding my own bloody business and still I seem a target for any perv and sicko who fancies their chances."

She shot Gabe a glance to indicate that she didn't entirely consider him exempt from this categorisation. He decided to go on the offensive, to lay before her what he knew about her involvement in the murder that was plastered across all the papers.

"Hmm, maybe it's got something to do with the murder," he said, getting progressively angrier and red in the face, "You know, the one at the National Gallery that everybody's talking about. The one where you were seen fleeing the scene of the crime. The one where the victim drew the symbol on your tattoo onto the wall. Maybe, it's something to do with that."

"How the bloody hell do you know what's on my tattoos?" she said equally angrily, she was wearing a leather jacket today that completely covered her arms so the symbol was not visible, "Or that I witnessed the murder? How long have you been following me for, freak?"

Gabe hadn't been expecting this level of aggressive defensiveness or these counter accusations. Still, he knew that he had to keep up the pressure, he could be close to discovering the truth.

"So, you don't deny it then?" he countered, "That the symbol on your tattoo matches the one the victim drew on the wall?"

"Which tattoo? What are you talking about?"

He grabbed her jacket and yanked it open and half way down her arm, revealing the bare skin and some of her different tattoos. On her left upper arm, he saw the circle and the cross he was looking for. As he leaned in for a closer look, she hit him. It was a forceful punch that landed square on his jaw and sent him back to the other side of the taxi.

"Back off, creep," she said, both of them now as confrontational as each other.

"There!" he pointed at the inked design on her arm and demanded accusingly "That's the one. Just the same as the dead girl drew. What is it? What does it mean? Some sort of conspiracy? A secret order?"

"Ha!" she laughed loudly in his face, her anger seeming mixed with genuine mirth, "That!" she pointed at her arm, jabbing the symbol with her index finger, "That is the symbol for female, you idiot! It means womanhood. Feminism. That's your secret fucking society. The international conspiracy of womankind not to be molested by creeps in the back of cabs!"

Gabe backed off. His mind was spinning with thoughts. Now that he looked again at the completely uncovered tattoo, he could tell that it wasn't quite the same as the symbol drawn in blood. The circle with a cross beneath it was all there was, the dead woman's symbol had an arrow pointing from the other side of the circle. He didn't know what to think. The main reason for his suspicions over this woman had just been blown out of the water and yet she had just been attacked in public by a couple of thugs clearly after her for something.

"Look. I...I'm sorry," he said, his confrontational tone now replaced by a more conciliatory one, "I just saw the tattoo and the symbol in the blood and they just seemed similar and you, well you seemed out of place in a museum, so I just kind of thought that maybe there was a link or something."

"What symbol in the blood?" she replied, frustrated, not following his train of thought, "What are you talking about?"

Gabe sighed, he was beginning to realise that this woman was as clueless as he was about the murder. Either that or she was a very cunning and deceptive actress. He decided to let her in on his thinking, she was the only lead he had and he didn't intend to let it go even if it hadn't panned out as he had hoped.

"Look," he said, pulling out his laptop and bringing his photos up on the screen. Her aggression was now tempered with curiosity as she peered at the images, "There, this symbol here," he pointed at the close up on the blood drawing.

"Ha," she laughed again, "Not quite the same. Mine means womanhood. That's the transgender symbol."

"How do you know that?" he said, surprised and perhaps a little impressed.

"It's called an education," she said haughtily, her upper-class vowels becoming more pronounced with her patronising tone.

"OK, Miss Educated," Gabe replied, "That's what the symbol means, but what's it got to do with the murder? Or the National Gallery? The Rokeby Venus? Or those two thugs back there?"

"Now, you've got me there," she admitted, "I don't have the slightest bloody idea."

CHAPTER 2

Great, so it's the 'transgender symbol'," Gabe said, giving extra emphasis as he quoted her words as if they meant nothing to him, "That doesn't really bring us much closer to understanding."

"Us?" she said, now seeming genuinely quite amused rather than her previous threatened and threatening behaviour, "What us?"

"You're in this too now," Gabe said, seriously, "Our two ugly friends back there saw to that. The more we understand what's going on here, the more we can avoid ever having any contact with them again."

She seemed to consider this a valid point. She was beginning to relax a bit and put her guard down, beginning to trust that maybe Gabe wasn't a pervert or a stalker, that maybe he could be right.

"Fine," she shrugged acceptingly, "Well, I might not be able to figure out all this symbolism, but I know somebody who can." She turned to speak to the cabbie, "Can you take us to Cambridge, please?"

"Cambridge?!" said Gabe surprised.

"You gonna be able to afford that, love?" the driver asked.

"I have the money for it," the well-spoken punk said in her most aristocratic tones and the cab turned sharply around and headed away from the city.

"I'm Gabe, by the way," Gabe said, realising they hadn't introduced themselves, "Gabriel Herrison. I'm a photographer."

"Charmed," she said with a sharply ironic tone, "I'm Saphy."

"So..." Gabe said, unable to sit there in awkward silence any longer, "A transgender symbol, eh? What does that mean?"

After almost an hour and a half of feeling uncomfortable in the back of the cab with the fearsome stare of the purple haired punk eyeing him up from across the seat, Gabe was feeling pretty nervous. He had accepted that Saphy was probably as much in the dark as him about what had happened at the Gallery and about the guys that had chased them. That did not, however, make him any more comfortable in her company. Many times he felt on the verge of saying something only to have his ideas shot down by her withering look of contempt before he even had the chance to articulate them.

The huge urban sprawl of Greater London had been left long behind, to be replaced by the pleasant green fields of the English countryside. Driving into Cambridge put Gabe in a completely different place to the London he knew, a much smaller town with a much slower pace. People rode by the historic university buildings on bicycles and drove punts and rowing boats along the river.

Amongst these historic, academic scenes it was hard to imagine that they had recently been running for their lives and getting mixed up in a murder back in the city. Gabe began to relax and decided to raise some of the questions that had been on his mind for over an hour. Saphy, too, seemed to no longer be glaring at him quite so accusingly, as if she too had had a lot to think about on the way.

"What?" she replied, seemingly jogged by his question out of some deep thought, "What does it mean? You're asking what the symbolism of the shape is or what's the significance of it being drawn here? Because I can tell you the first, but I sure as hell don't have the faintest fucking clue about the other."

"No," Gabe confessed, "I meant what does that mean - - 'transgender'. It's not a word that I've ever heard before."

"Really?" Saphy scoffed, genuinely surprised, "You've never heard of transsexuals? You really are clueless aren't you? To think that you had me all scared back there, stalking me!" "So, what is a transgender or transsexual or whatever?" Gabe replied, a little frustrated.

"Somebody that's both genders, part man, part woman, in some way or another," said Saphy, picking her words carefully to clarify just what she felt about the subject, "They could be anything from crossdressers who just dress in clothing that isn't appropriate to their own gender, although girls seem to get away with this without such a stigma, to people with gender dysphoria who feel they are born into the wrong gendered body, some of which have been surgically altered to more closely resemble their real gender, if not completely surgically reassigned. Some are even born intersex, hermaphrodites with the genetic qualities of both sexes."

Gabe's heart skipped a beat at the sound of the word "hermaphrodite", something he had never heard mentioned by anyone but the book Love's Children and the visions in his dreams. He had never imagined that such people, part man, part woman, could ever exist in reality. It almost felt like fate, an idea and image that he had hardly thought about in years suddenly coming back in his dreams and then in reality too. However, Gabe was a pretty private person and wasn't about to open up about all this rush of feelings to a near total stranger, especially one he was still slightly scared of.

"You seem to know an awful lot about this," he said warily, instead, "You're not a..er..transsexual or something yourself, are you?"

"Screw you!" she responded aggressively, "That's just what people like you think, isn't it? That if you show any interest or understanding, then you're just one of 'them'! You know, I am actually capable of compassion and empathy toward other people. You should try it sometime."

"OK, OK, sorry," Gabe decided it was probably best not to bring up the thought of her tone right now not seeming all that compassionate, instead he decided to change the tack of the conversation, "So, what about that thing you said before, about the symbolism of the design here, the circle and the cross and the arrow. What can you tell me about that?" "It's a combination of the biological signs for male and female," Saphy replied, still slightly sullen, "My tattoo, as we've already established, is the female sign (see, if I was transgender, then my tattoo would have been just the same as the blood symbol). The male sign is a circle with an arrow coming from the top left."

"That seems pretty simple," Gabe said, glad to find, apart from her snarky aside, that Saphy had found a topic that would engage her in a more civil fashion.

"It's not," she said, seeming determined to contradict whatever he said, "People think that symbols are easy, like a code or an alphabet; this symbol means this, that one means that. But it's not true, the same shape of lines and circles can mean so many different things."

"How do you mean?"

"Imagine if my tattoo had this picture on it," she took a pen from where she saw it in Gabe's open laptop bag and drew a symbol on her arm, a hooked cross shape. Gabe recognised it instantly as the Nazi symbol, a swastika, "If that was my tattoo, you'd also have made some pretty quick judgements about what that tattoo said about me and my personality."

"That you're some mad, evil bitch," he responded, raising the hint of a smile on Saphy's lips for the first time.

"Exactly, but if you went back a couple of thousand years, then this same shape crops up frequently in Greek art and architecture, it's a sun symbol. Even today, it's still used as a symbol of harmony and balance in Hindu and Buddhist cultures. It actually guards against the kind of evil it has come to represent here in Europe. Of course, even knowing what it means to Buddhists, I could never bring myself to have that on my body," she spat on her arm and rubbed the ink off, "To us it will always now be a symbol of hate. But, others are not so set in stone."

Gabe was beginning to see that, like the symbols she was talking about, Saphy was a much more complicated prospect than she had first seemed. He had been quick to make judgements about her just like he had been quick to see the hooked swastika cross as a sign of evil. He was just starting to see that beneath that prickly persona was somebody who had picked up all kind of esoteric knowledge that could prove much more useful in unravelling the mystery that they were caught up in than any idea of his.

"So, your female sign doesn't just mean female?" he said.

"Exactly," Saphy agreed and Gabe let out an almost audible sigh to have found something that she finally agreed with, "It's actually the astrological symbol for the planet Venus and is a reference in itself to the goddess. Because Venus is the goddess of beauty and love, her object is the mirror. So, really the symbol originally represented a mirror. That's the glass surface," she pointed to the circle inked into her arm, "And that's the mirror's handle," she showed the cross, "So, I guess originally it was a symbol of female vanity, but, like I said, these meanings change over time. When the naturalist Linnaeus wanted to use symbols to represent male and female biological specimens, he chose the astrological symbol of Venus for female and Mars for male. Mars is the circle with an arrow coming out of it, it represents the war god's spear and shield. Basically, 18th century scientists had a really reductive idea of gender roles, even when it came to looking at plants, so men were warriors and women beauties."

"So, women really are from Venus and men are from Mars?"

"Don't be a dick," she replied, this time, however, smiling a little rather than spitting her response back aggressively, "Actually, that mirror thing reminds me," she went on, "This isn't the first time this painting's been attacked. In 1914 it was slashed as part of a protest by suffragettes after the arrest of Emmeline Pankhurst. They were trying hard to change the way women were perceived and I think they kind of objected to that image of lounging before a mirror, admiring our gorgeous reflections!"

"So, if it's a symbol of all those old fashioned ideas of women just needing to look good, being seen and not heard, why does it matter to you? Why have you got it permanently inked into your body?" Gabe felt he had to ask.

"Because, as I already told you, symbols' meanings can change," she responded, "These days feminists like to use it to show that we are proud of our womanhood. We don't want to be just like men, we are different and special and want to celebrate that. Those suffragettes did great things for their time, they allowed women to be who we are today, but that means we don't need to be like them any more. Yeah, we don't always want the image of being the vainer sex, but, come on, we're obviously the more attractive. So, maybe I don't mind being a little bit like Venus. There's nothing wrong with valuing beauty. And it is a beautiful painting, there's no denying that. I can't imagine ever wanting to damage such a lovely thing as like they did."

"So, if your tattoo is the symbol for women and beauty and Venus, then why is that not the one that was written in blood on the gallery wall?" Gabe was beginning to feel that Saphy was using the discussion more as a chance to air her opinions than really answer the questions they needed answering, "Why this transgender one instead, Venus and Mars together in one?" "Honestly? I have absolutely no idea," Saphy confessed, directing her eyes to the ground, for once no longer staring right at Gabe, her strident, opinionated tones somewhat suppressed to sound, for almost the first time, as if the real her was coming out a little.

"Look," she went on, "You were right, what you said before about being in this together, and needing to understand what we're dealing with after what happened back in London. I don't like it at all, but you're right. I don't know any of the answers, but I'm taking you to the one person I know who might be able to help."

Seemingly on cue, at this point, the cab driver turned back to face them.

"Sorry to interrupt your little lecture, love," he said, "But we're here. Cambridge. Now, where is it I can leave you?"

"Pembroke College," Saphy's voice had resumed it's plummy, upper-class tone of command, making it clear that her moment of confiding in Gabe was long since over, however he was surprised to hear her then add, "I hate this place. Just a world of traditionalist, elitist, smug idiots."

Pembroke College is one of Cambridge's oldest and best regarded. As the cab pulled up on Trumpington Street, Gabe and Saphy were confronted with the building's impressive historical façade. The chapel, designed by the legendary architect Christopher Wren, is a neat, elegant, classically styled building that drew Gabe's attention momentarily as they walked passed it and under a rather imposing mediaeval gatehouse.

Above the gates, two windows looked out from either side of a coat of arms, giving the whole thing the impression of a frowning disapproving face, with the gates making up the downturned mouth and the windows narrow eyes, looking with disgust at the awkward young man and his tattooed purple haired accomplice who dared to enter the hallowed grounds of the prestigious college.

Inside the college grounds, Gabe followed Saphy along paths through exquisitely manicured lawns and tall plane trees. Gabe didn't ask where they were going, but Saphy seemed to know just where to head. Even though she seemed even more out of place than he did amongst these sedate, traditional surroundings, the gothic architecture of the buildings quite different from the gothic style of her leather and biker boots, Gabe could see that all this was pretty familiar to her.

They headed for a Victorian building with tall brick chimneys and went inside. The corridors were rather less grand than they looked on the outside. The walls were plain white plaster with a number of simple looking doors each with a little plaque telling you which doctor or professor had which office. Saphy strode ahead, seeming anxious to get through all this, her heavy boots clumping along the wood floor. She stopped at a door and knocked.

"This is it," she grimaced, "We're here."

The plaque on this particular door read "Professor Jane Cavendish -- Transgender Studies". A voice sounded from inside, inviting them in. Saphy opened the door and Gabe followed her inside. Professor Cavendish was sat behind her desk, reading. As they came in, she looked up and registered Saphy's presence with a look of recognition and surprise.

The office was crowded with books, there were shelves from floor to ceiling with books arranged in a seemingly random order, along the shelf and then lying on top as well. The desk was also spread with books and papers leaving very little space of desk itself. The window behind the desk gave a pleasant view of the green lawn outside. There were a couple of pictures hanging on the wall. One showed an ancient feast day, as the men and women lounged around a table of food a shower of pink rose petals fell on them. The other showed a knight in full armour except for a helmet, sat staring out to sea, with long flowing blonde hair and a somewhat androgynous face.

Jane Cavendish herself was a woman of indeterminate age. Her long waves of hair were already mostly grey, but her smooth skin and bright eyes suggested the greying was a little premature and that Professor Cavendish was actually quite young to have got to such a position of respect. She was not necessarily attractive, but Gabe's photographer's eye saw a face that was definitely interesting, striking even. She wore a pair of old fashioned horn rimmed spectacles that sat on the end of her nose as she looked over them at Saphy.

"Persephone Cross!" she exclaimed, "I didn't expect to see you back here again. Not ever, and certainly not so soon."

"I'm not back," Saphy said, "Well, not for good. We have a little problem. A mystery and I think you're the only one who can help."

"She was my best student," Professor Cavendish explained, turning to Gabe, "The brightest and most eager to learn."

"Was?" Gabe asked.

"Oh yes, you're looking at a certified college dropout," Saphy smirked.

"And who's your friend, Miss Cross?" Professor Cavendish looked Gabe up and down, sizing him up and trying to place him, to figure out where he fitted in the world of her aggressive purple haired feminist former student.

"This...This isn't a friend," she replied, "I don't know, we just met this morning. Although he seems to have been following me for longer," here she shot Gabe an accusing look, "We were witnesses to a murder and I think somebody wants us out of the way."

"That sounds pretty melodramatic, Saphy," Professor Cavendish, "What on earth makes you think that?"

Saphy sighed as if she had hoped she wouldn't have to go through the whole story with her old professor. She came over to the desk and took a seat, feeling that they were set to be there for a while. After a few seconds, Gabe joined her in the other chair that sat opposite.

"You've seen the news about the murder at the National Gallery?" Saphy said.

"Ah yes, the Rokeby Venus, wasn't it?" Professor Cavendish replied, "You were there?" "That's right, me and Gabe here, we saw the whole thing. We wanted to get your take on it."

"I assume you've considered this painting being targeted for the same reasons as in 1914, Slasher Mary," she said the name with a sense of disdain, "That's if the painting itself has any significance at all. You must have more than this to go on if you thought I could help."

"I told you before that somebody wants us out of the way, I wasn't exaggerating," Saphy replied, "This morning I was attacked by a couple of really sinister guys, proper criminal types not some random muggers. Coming so soon after witnessing such an unusual murder, I just don't think it can be a coincidence."

"We hoped that if we can figure out the mystery, we can avoid that happening to us again, maybe get the police to protect us if we can give them any real information," Gabe chipped in, "Hopefully you can help us a little there." "So, what have you got that made you think of me?" Professor Cavendish asked, "Not that it's not nice that I'm still on your mind, Saphy."

"What can you tell us about this?" Gabe said, showing her the photo on his laptop screen, the woman with her arm outstretched, daubing her own blood on the wall in the shape of the transgender symbol, the mix of Venus and Mars.

"Hmmm, now that's something they've kept out of the papers," the professor responded, "That is interesting. Yes, I can tell you quite a bit about this symbol and how it relates to the painting. You were right to assume some kind of connection. I don't know, though, how much I can help with solving your murder, but I'll tell you what I know."

"What do you know about Hermaphroditus in graecoroman mythology?" Professor Cavendish asked.

"I know the poem," Saphy replied, quoting, "'Lift up thy lips, turn round, look back for love, blind love that comes by night and casts out rest.' 'To what strange end hath some strange god made fair the double blossom of two fruitless flowers?'"

"Ah, Swinburne, how very decadent," Professor Cavendish smiled.

"Who's Swinburne?" Gabe inquired.

"Algernon Swinburne," the professor explained, "Something of a controversial, scandalous poet in the Victorian age. He wrote about homosexuality and sadomasochism and a lot of other less seemly subjects.

Most famously, he wrote about your companion's near namesake and heroine, the Greek poet Sappho."

"'I feel thy blood against my blood; my pain Pains thee, and lips bruise lips, and vein stings vein. Let fruit be crushed on fruit, let flower on flower Breast kindle breast, and either burn one hour,'" came Saphy's quoting voice once more, "He writes so sensually about the force of desire in Sappho for another woman." "Well, maybe, but Swinburne wasn't the first nor the last person to write about Hermaphroditus," Professor Cavendish went on.

"Love's Children," said Gabe, much to the surprise of the two women, "The story of Hermaphroditus was in that. He went swimming in the stream of a nymph called Salmacis and she wanted him so badly that she dived in too and grabbed him, not letting go until their bodies became one. And the stream is supposed to be cursed to bring the same transformation on people who swim there or drink it."

"Wow, that was unexpected," Saphy replied, "And you gave the impression that you knew nothing at all about classics, art and mythology."

"It was one of my favourite books as a child," Gabe blushed.

"You know that Robert White teaches here at Pembroke," Professor Cavendish, "Or taught, rather."

"What happened?" "He just disappeared," she replied, "He was always heading off around the world on one wild archaeological goose chase or another. Finally, a few months ago, he left on a trip and hasn't come back since."

"That's a shame, it would have been good to get his opinion too," Gabe said.

"I don't know how much you'd have got out of him," Professor Cavendish told him, "He never wanted to talk about Love's Children. It was his only attempt at a fictional book and its failure was really devastating to him. He was always a bit strange after that." She paused for a moment, lost in thought, before going on, "Anyway, Gabe, you're right. The story in White's book is the story usually told about Hermaphroditus. It's mostly forgotten today, but in classical times the figure of Hermaphroditus was a common, popular one."

She went over to her huge shelves full of books and browsed along their spines until she pulled down a few that caught her interest. Sitting back down at the desk, she opened one of the books, The Hermaphrodite in Classical Art, and opened a page in the middle of the book with big glossy photographs of Greek statues. They resembled the usual style of classical statues of beautiful, elegant goddesses except in one detail. One showed a tall beautiful woman in a heroic pose with a robe draped over her shoulder, it dropped away at the front to reveal her naked breasts and, between her legs, a small but perfectly sculpted penis. Another almost cheekily raised up the skirt of her flowing dress to reveal a similar penis beneath it.

"Images like these were very popular with the ancient Greeks. They appreciated things that seemed strange or unusual and their attitudes to sexuality and gender were much freer than many people's today. The birth of a hermaphrodite was thought to be something divine and a good omen of things to come," Professor Cavendish explained, "They saw the union of male and female as something special and complete. In fact the image of the hermaphrodite was often used as being symbolic of a marriage, the idea being that marriage is the perfect union of man and woman into one whole. The married couple as one individual rather than two." "But Hermaphroditus and Salmacis were hardly a perfect union in the legend," Gabe said, "It's more like she raped him!"

"Quite," Professor Cavendish replied.

"It's actually pretty rare in graeco-roman mythology to have the woman rape the man," Saphy said, "There's loads the other way, nice to see the balance redressed a little!"

"Anyway, the popularity of the hermaphrodite in art and legend kind of went into decline after the end of the Roman Empire," Professor Cavendish continued, "You don't really see any images like these during the mediaeval period. However, suddenly, in the renaissance they become popular again. In the 16th century writers like Edmund Spenser and Philip Sidney wrote some of the major works of English poetry containing characters crossdressed and acting like the other gender. Of course, this is the age of boys dressing as girls to act on the stage. Just look at Shakespeare's plays, all the female parts would have been played by boys. In quite a lot of the plays these female characters then disguise themselves as boys once more. So, you've got boys playing girls playing boys. Obviously people in that age were interested in how fluid gender roles could be.

"This was also an age of new scientific interest in people being born intersex. In 1573, the French surgeon Ambroise Pare wrote about hermaphrodites in his On Monsters and Prodigies. In 1612, the Swiss botanist Gaspard Bauhin wrote On the Nature of the Births of Hermaphrodites and Monsters, complete with illustrations that recalled the classical beauty of the ancient hermaphrodite statues. In the same year, a woman condemned to death as a lesbian was given a reprieve because she was a hermaphrodite and, therefore, could legitimately claim to be male."

"I know all this already, Jane," Saphy said, a little frustrated, "This was all on your course."

"Yes, it's all very interesting," Gabe agreed, "But I don't see what it has to do with the Venus painting." "I'm getting to that, have a little patience," Professor Cavendish gently chided. She took another book from the pile on her desk and opened it to another glossy photo of a statue, "The real thing that made the legend of Hermaphroditus particularly popular in the 1600s was this. It's a Roman copy of a bronze statue by Polycles, a Greek sculptor about 150 years before the birth of Christ. The statue was lost for centuries, but in around 1600 it was rediscovered in Rome when digging for the foundations of the church of Santa Maria della Vittoria. The Cardinal Scipione Borghese, a man with a huge amount of power in the church, an art collector rumoured to have been gay, took ownership of the statue, which became known as the Borghese Hermaphroditus. It was an image that was hugely popular and much reproduced over the next few decades. It's now on display in the Louvre in Paris."

"So?" Gabe asked.

Professor Cavendish turned the open page of her book around on the desk so Gabe and Saphy could see the image of the statue. Beside it, she opened a second book, Venus in Renaissance Art, with a glossy reproduction of the Rokeby Venus, an image that had embedded itself into Gabe's mind over the past few days.

"Look familiar?" she asked.

She was right. The image of the Borghese Hermaphroditus showed the statue of what appeared to be a beautiful woman viewed from behind. She was reclining, lying on her side slightly propped up on her elbow with her head raised above this, emphasising the curve of the narrow waist and wide hips. It was the exact same posture as that of Venus in the painting. However, while the painting could only be viewed from that one angle, with the statue the other side was visible in another reproduced image and that showed the beautiful reclining feminine figure to have a penis resting between her thighs.

"So, what you're saying is... " Gabe began

"The secret of the Rokeby Venus is that she isn't Venus at all," Professor Cavendish confirmed, "It's a painting of Hermaphroditus!" "Velazquez was a very smart painter and his paintings are full of complex symbolism that critics still argue about today," Professor Cavendish explained, "In particular, there are quite a few aspects of the Rokeby Venus that scholars struggle to interpret. As you know, the mirror is the symbol of Venus and she is often painted with one, however it is a mystery why Velazquez chose a composition where she faces away from us, with the reflection in the mirror indistinct and vague. Equally, the symbolism of the winged Cupid figure is a matter for some debate. Why is he holding up the mirror to Venus? What is the significance of the red ribbon in his hand?

"The mirror and the figure of Cupid are the reasons why the image has been consistently identified as being Venus. However, there is enough doubt about this to trouble scholars. The painting shows none of the other paraphernalia that usually allow us to identify an image of Venus. There are no roses or myrtle, the plants commonly associated with the goddess.

"Also, more significantly, she is a brunette. Not that significant, you might say, but look at every other contemporary and earlier image of Venus. Her blonde hair is the single defining characteristic that runs through them. She is even known in mythology as Venus Aurea, Golden Venus."

She turned the pages of the book to show earlier images of the goddess. There was the one of her emerging from the sea with her flowing golden locks that Gabe remembered so well from the cover of Love's Children. Another showed her reclining with a posy of flowers in her hand, unlike the Velazquez, she was facing straight toward us, nude with her body fully, sensually on show. In another, a bulkier, less slender Venus admired herself in a mirror, except unlike the Velazquez, the reflection was clear and distinct. One thing running through all of these paintings was the goddess' golden hair.

"So, maybe it isn't Venus," Gabe said, "But if it isn't, then why is it Hermaphroditus?"

"And why are Cupid and the mirror, always associated with Venus, in the picture if it isn't her?" Saphy added.

"And why the need for all this secrecy and symbolism?" Gabe asked, "Why not just paint an image of Hermaphroditus?"

"Because the 17th century Spain that Velazquez came from was a place of moral and religious repression and intolerance," Professor Cavendish replied, "The Inquisition was at the height of its powers. Although the image of Hermaphroditus and the idea of bending gender rules was popular elsewhere in Europe and even among the Spanish aristocracy, Velazquez would have had trouble with some of the Catholic church had he painted just what he wanted.

"Many people's argument for why the figure of Venus faces the other way from us is that, under the Inquisition, the Spanish government had strongly discouraged the painting of nudes. In fact, if the painting was done from life, as it seems from the sensual realism of it, then it would surely have been painted from a male model, as Velazquez would not have been allowed a female nude to paint from.

"The painting was probably done in about 1650, during a time when Velazquez was in Italy, slightly freer to paint as he wished than he would be in Spain under the Inquisition. The legend of the Borghese Hermaphroditus was such that the King of Spain asked Velazquez to have a bronze copy cast. Velazquez, therefore, must have spent a fair bit of time around the sculpture while he was painting the Rokeby Venus, which would account for the similarity in posture. Maybe that time awakened an interest in Hermaphroditus and the legend enough to influence the subject of Velazquez's painting."

"But, maybe he just used the shape of the statue's pose to inspire him," Gabe suggested.

"Looking at it now, the pose isn't quite so exactly the same as it first seemed," Saphy added, beginning to doubt the truth in what her former professor had said.

"Like many other works of this period, it's been retouched and restored a few times down the years," Professor Cavendish responded, "The shape of the arm and head has been altered, the head used to turn more to the left. The original shape, closer to the Hermaphroditus sculpture, has only been apparent recently using infra-red.

"Velazquez himself probably made some of these changes. Perhaps he felt that the similarity with the Hermaphroditus statue he was having copied at the same time was too obvious. Interestingly, the area around the left foot seems unfinished. However, it appears to be deliberate, almost as if Velazquez is making some symbolic point about the left foot. Once again, however, nobody can agree on what that point is.

"As for further reasons why the painting is Hermaphroditus, he is the only character who isn't Venus herself that fits the symbolism of the other objects, Cupid, the mirror and the ribbon. If we assume the painting not to be Venus, then Hermaphroditus is the only other logical choice. Cupid, like Hermaphroditus, was the son of Venus and the two of them are often compared.

"In the original Salmacis legend, the nymph's first thoughts on seeing Hermaphroditus are that he must be Cupid himself. Many of the artistic representations painted on vases that these books speculate to be Hermaphroditus are often identified instead as Cupid. He is even often referred to as 'a second Cupid'. So, that would explain why Cupid is holding up a mirror to him, they are mirrors of each other."

"And the ribbons?" Saphy asked.

"They have often been thought to symbolise blind love," the professor explained, "Often in art Cupid is depicted as blind with ribbons around his eyes. There is a legend about how Cupid became blind that I think is relevant to the picture here. It appears in Francis Beaumont's poem Salmacis and Hermaphroditus. Beaumont was a playwright who worked for a short time with Shakespeare. His first work, around the time of the discovery of the Borghese Hermaphroditus statue was this epic poem retelling the Salmacis legend. Here, I'll read a section to you: '"His eyes were Cupid's, for until his birth, Cupid had eyes, and lived upon the earth, Till on a day, when the great Queen of love Was by her white doves drawn from heaven above, Unto the top of the Idalian hill, To see how well the Nymphs their charge fulfil, And whether they had done the goddess right, In nursing of her sweet Hermaphrodite: Whom when she saw, although complete and full, Yet she complained, his eyes were somewhat dull: And therefore, more the wanton boy to grace, She pulled the sparkling eyes from Cupid's face, Feigning a cause to take away his sight, Because the Ape would sometimes shoot for spite. But Venus set those eyes in such a place, As graced those clear eyes with a clearer face.'

"In the painting, the blurry image of Hermaphroditus' face in the mirror as Cupid holds it up, his ribbons of blindness draped over it, refer to how his brother has taken his shining eyes for himself.

"So, that's it. That's the secret of the Rokeby Venus and that's the significance of the transgender sign beneath it. I know that may have cleared up one mystery for you, but I don't think it gets you any closer to understanding the murder. I can't imagine somebody would kill to prevent an old secret coded in a classic painting from being revealed, especially when academics like me have already put forward these theories to universal disinterest."

"Yes, I can't imagine this is really information the police are going to take all that seriously," Saphy agreed, "We can't ask for protection from mysterious assassins because a painting of a goddess is really a guy!"

"It's a shame Robert White isn't around," Gabe added, "I'd have liked to see what he had to say."

"You could swing by his office anyway," Professor Cavendish suggested, "His colleague, Dr. Gerard should be there. He may be able to give you some pointers on Professor White's research."

As they left Professor Cavendish's office, both Gabe and Saphy felt a little disappointed. Of course, they had learnt a lot, but much of it didn't seem immediately relevant to a problem that could threaten their lives.

Would somebody kill to protect a painting's secret? Why? And would they do it again?

Gabe knew that he wanted to speak to this Dr. Gerard, but Saphy didn't seem sure about that suggestion.

"I think I'd rather head to the library," she said, "There's one of the best libraries in the world here. If there's anything that might give us a clue why the painting's hermaphrodite secret is worth killing over, it's there," she paused for a moment, about to head off in the opposite direction, "Listen, I'm getting out of here by this evening. With those guys potentially on my tail, I don't want to stay in any place longer than I have to, especially not here," she looked around her with barely disguised disdain, "Meet me at the train station by seven. If you're not there, I'm leaving without you."

With that, Saphy turned and walked away, her heavy boots still slamming against the pavement. She was obviously not feeling relaxed, she kept brushing and tossing her purple hair out of her eyes. Gabe got the impression that perhaps she had only headed in the opposite direction from a need to be alone with her thoughts. Well, maybe Gabe would be better off pursuing things alone as well. Her opinionated presence wouldn't really be necessary when meeting another professor.

Gabe knocked on the door marked "Professor Robert White, Dr. Raymond Gerard -- Classics", and listened for an answer. He heard nothing from inside the office. It was already late in the afternoon of what had seemed a long day. That morning he had been in London retracing his steps on the day of the murder, going back to the National Gallery. That certainly seemed a lot more than a few hours ago. Since then he'd been caught up in even more violence and mystery and found himself investigating arcane mythology long thought lost in the dreams of childhood.

He knocked again and still heard nothing but silence. He tried the door and it opened without resistance. The office was empty for the moment. Gabe knew that it was impolite and invasive, but he still found himself going in for a look around. Robert White had written the one book that had affected him more than any other, he was curious about what this man was really like.

In the office, there were two desks, and stacks of bookshelves and filing cabinets, just like Professor Cavendish's office. However, here the space was clearly shared by two quite different characters. One desk had a mess of files and paper work spread out all over it. The other was neat and clean. Gabe headed for the messy desk. Sure enough, this was the one with a name plaque reading Robert White.

CHAPTER 3

Knowing full well that this level of snooping wasn't really acceptable behaviour, but filled with a desire to know more about the professor's disappearance, Gabe went over to the desk and began to look through the messy pile of books and papers. He was desperate to discover anything he could that might tell him something about Robert White and the story of Hermaphroditus that White had written and that had so much held sway over Gabe's childhood imagination.

Looking through all the papers revealed very little that Gabe could very well understand. The writing was scrawled in lines so close together that it was virtually illegible in places, while in others individual words were so spread out that it was hard to see which words went with which. There were pictures that looked like vague doodles and lists of strange names from mythology and place names, lines drawn all over maps of the Mediterranean.

Suddenly, he stumbled across something that made his heart skip a beat, a familiar beautiful naked reclining figure, reproduced in blurry black and white but clearly the Borghese Hermaphroditus. There was a list scrawled in the same messy handwriting beneath the picture. It read -- "Louvre, Paris; Villa Borghese, Rome; Palazzo Massimo Alle Terme, Rome; Vatican, Rome; Uffizi, Florence; Prado, Madrid; Met, New York". The bottom part of the list had been torn away. Gabe folded it up and slipped it into his pocket just as he heard footsteps and the office door opening.

"Excuse me, you appear to be in my office, uninvited," came a voice with a commanding and slightly annoyed tone, "What are you looking for?"

Gabe turned to see a man of about fifty, his hair thinning, combed over to cover his baldness in an act of unsuccessful vanity. Apart from that point, he seemed well kept and in good physical condition for a middle-aged academic. His suit was well tailored and immaculately neat. He stared at Gabe in a way that seemed a little condescending, but he was obviously taking meticulous note of every detail of what he saw.

Gabe could tell that he was in the presence of a man with an obviously keen intellect and bright observational faculties.

"Dr. Gerard?" Gabe guessed, "I've come looking for Robert White."

"You wouldn't be the first," was all that Dr. Gerard responded, "He hasn't been seen in months."

"I was wondering if you could help me," Gabe went on, "Tell me about some of Professor White's research. I've been talking to Professor Cavendish, she told me you might be able to show me some of Professor White's ideas."

"Robert had plenty of pretty eccentric ideas," Dr. Gerard said, his eyes scanning where Gabe had been going through the papers on White's desk, "I guess you can see that his mind was never the most organised. Recently, things had been getting much worse. He always saw himself as something of an adventurer, chasing after the truth in mythological ideas that so often wasn't there at all." "I read his book, Love's Children," Gabe went on.

"His great folly," Dr. Gerard replied, "As a young man, Robert thought that book would bring him fame and fortune, but the legends of the ancient world are of far more interest to fusty old academics like us than they ever will be for most of the public. Robert took its failure very hard. He was determined to seek out the truth in the legends, to show people why they should have been interested in the first place. When I first met him, almost thirty years ago, I found this drive inspiring. As the years we worked together went by, I found it more and more frustrating. There simply was too little historical evidence for a great many of Robert's fascinations and investigations. Before his disappearance, the college were considering cutting off us funding. He was starting to become something of an embarrassment."

"I was always interested in the story of Hermaphroditus in the book," Gabe said, "Was that becoming one of Professor White's pre-occupations? Did he think there was truth in the legend?" "It was never his first area of interest," Dr. Gerard replied, "But lately, in the months leading up to his disappearance, the idea of finding Salmacis was certainly one that he raised. It's preposterous of course."

"Salmacis? The nymph who became one body with Hermaphroditus?" Gabe said, curiously, "How could he think to find her?"

"Salmacis was the name of the fountain," Dr. Gerard explained, "The fountain whose waters were supposed to make men effeminate. Robert didn't ever believe that the stories he wrote about were completely true, the myths of gods and their children. However, he felt that they must have sprung from some original grain of real life, something the myth would grow up around. He thought that the Fountain of Salmacis, the waters that transform men's bodies, could exist in truth."

"Could it?" Gabe asked, excited by this thought far more than by anything he had learnt from Professor Cavendish, trying hard not to let this excitement burst out of him as he tried to process the idea that water that could turn men to women could really exist, "Could somebody still find the Fountain of Salmacis?"

"You'd better sit down," Dr. Gerard motioned to a seat beside his desk, "And I'll explain Robert's theories, and how wrong they could be."

Gabe crossed over from where he stood beside Professor White's desk, hoping that White's colleague hadn't noticed the slip of paper he had pocketed. Dr. Gerard's cold, clear eyes observed him minutely, seeming to think through just what to say to this naive, uneducated young man here to question him about his colleague's private business. As Gabe sat down on the other side of the desk, Dr. Gerard simply stared at him for a few seconds, before getting up and taking down some books from his shelves. It was almost the same action as Professor Cavendish had taken earlier, only Dr. Gerard's obviously meticulous classification system enabled him to find the books quicker. Gabe wondered to himself whether these academics could ever make any point without resorting to books for back-up.

"Robert used Ovid's Metamorphoses for much of the substance of his book," Dr. Gerard explained, after deciding what he felt worth divulging to Gabe, who he still looked upon somewhat patronisingly, "The Metamorphoses is pretty much the most influential Latin work on classical mythology, certainly in terms of the theme of love's influences and transformations. It's also the earliest extant version of the Hermaphroditus legend. It comes here in Book 4," here he opened the book onto the original story, "Ovid describes the story as a novelty, something that his audience would not have seen before. He probably invented it himself to explain the Hermaphroditus figure that was popular in the free standing sculpture of the time.

"However, it seems that the idea of the fountain that turned men into women was already in existence, even if the wider legend was not. This is how Ovid introduces his story:

"'How Salmacis, with weak enfeebling streams,'" he quoted, "'Softens the body, and unnerves the limbs, And what the secret cause, shall here be shown; The cause is secret, but the effect is known.'" "So, the nymph rapist is a myth, but there is really a Fountain of Salmacis?" Gabe asked, unable to suppress all of the thrill that he felt at this idea.

"It certainly appears as a story in some of the more respected writers of the day, but most even then were happy to dismiss it as idle fancy," Dr. Gerard confirmed, "Strabo's Geographica, pretty much the best guide to the places and cultures of the classical world," he said decisively, opening another book and searching for the right section, "Here we are, Book 14, he describes the fountain as having 'the slanderous repute, for what reason I do not know, of making effeminate all who drink from it. It seems that the effeminacy of man is laid to the charge of the air or of the water; yet it is not these, but rather riches and wanton living, that are the cause of effeminacy.'

"Vitruvius' De architectura, the great Roman treatise on architecture," he went on, opening a second book, "In Book 2, Vitruvius says: 'There is a mistaken idea that this spring infects those who drink of it. It cannot be that the water makes men effeminate.' You see, most of these writers feel the legend is just that, a legend, which does not stand up to much close scrutiny."

"But Professor White believed it was real," Gabe cut in, "He believed he could find it."

"Robert was like that," Dr. Gerard sighed, "He always believed in the truth behind the legend. He would feel that stories would never have grown up around that fountain had it not had some transformative properties. He spent his life following up these stories and never found anything worth mentioning."

"But, maybe he's right," Gabe said, "How would the legend have started without there being some grain of truth in it?"

"It's just as Strabo said, effeminate behaviour could stem from wanton living," Dr. Gerard replied, disapprovingly, "Then it would be easy for people to blame this debauchery on the waters rather than allowing people to take responsibility for it themselves."

"So, do any of these old scholars say where the fountain was supposed to be?" Gabe asked, slightly impatiently.

"Strabo puts it next to the Mausoleum at Halicarnassus," came the response, "One of the Seven Wonders of the World," he added patronisingly, after a pause in which he did not register any recognition in Gabe for this ancient site, "It was in Asia Minor, Turkey today."

"So, why didn't Professor White just go there?"

"The Mausoleum is no longer there," Dr. Gerard explained with a little frustration, "It was destroyed in an earthquake hundreds of years ago. During the crusades most of the stone was used elsewhere. Even if we did know exactly where the Fountain of Salmacis was supposed to be, it would all be ruins by now."

He paused momentarily to let this information sink in, then seemed to decide that this information brought an end to his conversation with Gabe, seemed to feel that he had more important things to be getting on with.

"I'm sure I would be interested to discuss Robert's research further, but I'm a busy man," he said, "I'm afraid that I've got a lot of work to be getting on with. Please, come back and see me some other time if you have any further questions."

With that, he seemed to completely block out Gabe's presence, opening a file full of papers on his desk and beginning to read through them as Gabe got up and headed for the door. However, just as Gabe was about to leave, Dr. Gerard gave him one final parting shot.

"The last time I saw Robert, he told me had discovered some of the waters of the Fountain of Salmacis," he said, stopping a shocked Gabe in his tracks, "He also told me that they had no transformative affect. It was nothing but regular water. It's a myth, Mr. Herrison, a myth with no basis in fact."

In spite of these last remarks, Gabe left the office in excitable spirits. He couldn't help imagining the fountain that turned men feminine could be real just like in Professor White's book. Perhaps the Fountain of Salmacis was something that really could be found again. Perhaps legends and myths could be proved true. If only the clues could be followed.

Instinctively Gabe knew that a secret like the discovery of the Fountain of Salmacis was just the kind of thing somebody would be willing to protect by any means, even if that meant hurting people. Even if that meant killing them. He had always had a tendency of jumping to conclusions, drawing links in an imaginary chain from the most tenuous connections, and now his mind went into overdrive doing just that. He let his childhood fascination with Hermaphroditus run away with him as he tried to fit the mystery together. Logically, there was nothing particularly to connect the murder in front of the Rokeby Venus, it's secret identity as Hermaphroditus, the disappearance of Robert White and his search for the Fountain of Salmacis, but logic had little part to play in Gabe's excitement.

To Gabe's mind, the coincidental return of his mind to Love's Children and Hermaphroditus at the time of the murder seemed like fate leading him on. He felt that the symbol on the wall had been drawn just so the painting's secret would be revealed and lead him on to discover an even greater secret. A part of him felt that seeing the goddess herself in his dreams that night was a sign that lead him on down this path. That these were just the same instincts that had Saphy pegged as the murderer in his mind just from looking at her picture didn't seem to bother Gabe right then.

Indeed, he was completely lost in these thoughts as he walked back through the pleasantly manicured lawns of this historic college grounds. A light, misty drizzle had begun to form as Gabe exited the frowning gatehouse and headed back onto the street, but he barely noticed the weather. Nor did he pay any attention to the way that the shadow of the gatehouse that loomed over him seemed to shift away from the light, so deep was he inside his own mind.

The touch of a cold hand digging claw-like into his shoulder shook Gabe uncomfortably from his reveries, bringing him crashing back down to the dangerous reality in which he now found himself. Two long, tall figures loomed over him, grabbed tight onto his arms giving him no chance to struggle. A high pitched hissing voice came almost straight into his mind, seeming to emanate from both shapes in unison.

"This time, there will be no escape," it hissed, "You will suffer so much more after what happened before. Now, we will make you truly know fear and dread."

Gabe felt a wave of terror and nausea run right through him. He felt light headed and numb with panic, unable to speak, barely able to move. He knew that with his slight, unmuscular frame, there was nothing he could do to escape the iron grip that held him from both sides. The inevitability of his imminent death weighed down on him until he could barely think straight.

To say his life flashed before his eyes would be an exaggeration, but he certainly got a sudden and unpleasant sense of how little he had done with his short life. He felt the sharp point of a knife blade pressed against his back and hoped that his end would come quickly and without pain.

The knife dug in deeper and he felt warm blood running down his body. This wasn't going to be quick at all. They were going to make him suffer, make him feel the pain. A third shape loomed out of the shadows and the knife blade stopped digging into him.

Gabe looked up in relief and felt a crashing blow come down against his temple. His mind slid into blackness, his last thought as his body hit the floor was the seeming certain knowledge that he would never wake up again in this world.

Professor Jane Cavendish slammed the door of her small one bedroom flat. She kicked off her shoes and let her heavy shoulder bag fall to the floor. It had been quite a day. She had been confronted by murder, mystery and the return into her life or someone she had thought lost.

When she had first seen the reports of the Rokeby Venus murder, Jane had to admit that her thoughts had instantly gravitated towards her own fascination with the painting, her own theories. She had published a paper on the secret symbolism of the Rokeby Venus a few years earlier and it had attracted very little attention, yet the first thing she thought of when the painting appeared in the news was that it was related to her discoveries.

Like any rationally thinking person, however, Jane had dismissed this as projecting her own preoccupations onto the news story. And then her prodigal departed best student had walked back into her office and confronted her with the grisly symbolism she had espoused written in blood at the murder scene. It was really something to take in.

Saphy Cross had always been a troubled girl, set somewhat apart from the rest of the bright young things in Jane's classes, pretty, preppy kids brimming with confidence, keen to get ahead in the world. Saphy was different. Beneath that fiery exterior, brimming with piercings and tattoos, full of aggression, was a smart and sensitive girl who had never really had anyone to look out for her.

Saphy had learned to think for herself and to never take anybody else's opinion as truth. It had meant that she was always coming out with smart new ideas that hadn't even occurred to Jane, but that she was a nightmare to teach anything and get her to accept it without hundreds of questions. She was just the kind of student to frustrate any teacher and just the kind that the best teachers truly remember.

Jane knew that Saphy came from a fairly privileged background and had had all the benefits of an expensive private education. She also knew that the girl had a lot of troubles back home. She had obviously fallen out pretty seriously with her family. After a few months in which Jane felt she and Saphy had got close enough for Saphy to open up, she had tried to get Saphy to elaborate on her home situation, but the younger woman had just returned to her prickly former self.

She also knew that Saphy did not easily form bonds with the other students, her concerns were not the same as theirs. She knew that Saphy seemed unhappy with life in Cambridge and yet she was still shocked when Saphy had completely dropped out. She had mentioned no such doubts to Jane and Jane had felt a little hurt that her student did not consider her suitably wise or supportive to turn to for advice. She had felt that they had a connection, that under her guidance the smart, brilliant talents of the younger woman could have flourished. Instead, Saphy had just disappeared until that afternoon.

If she had been surprised and disappointed by Saphy's sudden departure, the professor was even more surprised by her former student's reappearance that afternoon, and by the story she had to tell. She had not lied when she had said that it was nice that she was still in Saphy's thoughts. She still hoped that the girl would make something of herself. She hoped that her appearance once more in Jane's office would signal her return to Pembroke, even though she quickly saw that was a false hope. However, even to talk with her on Jane's favourite subject for that one afternoon made her feel good. She was pleased to see Saphy remained interested and sharp, whatever new trouble she was getting into.

She had known Saphy get into more than her fair share of scrapes in Cambridge, but this seemed in a whole different league. A woman was dead and, if Saphy was to be believed, she could prove to be the next target. Jane knew that Saphy felt she could handle herself most of the time, so to ask for help like this she must be pretty worried. To team up with another person was equally unusual for her. Saphy's companion had not at first seemed much to Jane, a pale skinny boy with not a lot of brains, but the professor had begun to suspect that he too had a few hidden depths. However things went, she was pleased that Saphy had this boy tagging along with her. Something, however, was still troubling her and she could not quite put her finger on it.

Deciding to clear her head in the hope of dislodging whatever it was that lurked troublingly at the back of her mind, Jane headed across her living room, as lined with books as her office, and into the bathroom. She turned the taps until they ran warm and flicked the switch to make the warm water run from her shower. She slipped out of her skirt and blouse, leaving them in a messy heap on the floor, and stepped under the running water of the shower.

As she pushed her greying hair back from her face and let the warm water snake through it, dripping down onto her back, Jane felt her anxious mental jumble untangle. Her mind began to clear and she felt able to think a bit more clearly. She relaxed as the shower's waters soothed her aching body, running in streams and rivulets over and around her fleshy curves.

Jane was proud of the shape her body was still in, she felt totally comfortable with the nakedness of the moment. She ran her hands over the warm mounds of her breasts, tracing the course of the water as the tributaries joined in a cascade between them, tumbling down her cleavage. Her hair dripped water down the small of her back until it converged over the curves of her backside, it ran down between her thighs and over that piece of flesh that was decidedly less feminine.

As Jane rubbed the soap suds into the feminine orbs of her breasts and down to the masculine rod of her penis, completely cleansing all parts and sides of her, she smiled to picture the image of herself. There she was, the body of a woman, still, she flattered herself, fairly decent looking, with the curves of chest and hips you would expect of a woman, but with the reproductive organs of a man. Standing beneath the cascading waters of the shower, she was the image of the legendary Hermaphroditus washed over by the waters of Salmacis' Fountain.

With that image, Jane felt her mind begin to focus on the detail of her earlier conversation that had been troubling her. Like many people, she did all of her best thinking in the shower, when she was able to just let all of herself be, without concealing or dressing it up. Now, under the falling water, she began to sort out the many disparate threads of her earlier thoughts. There was something about that symbol that was bothering her. Something that she had not remembered to tell Saphy and her friend.

She stepped out of the shower and wrapped herself in a warm, fluffy, comforting towel as her mind reached for that missing piece of the puzzle. It was the image of Hermaphroditus that made her think of it. The symbol she had identified was the transgender symbol. She had seen it time and time again in both her personal and professional life and yet it seemed wrong here.

A sound from the next room momentarily broke her chain of thought. Still dressed in just a towel, Jane went back through from her bathroom to the living room, all the while deep in thought. The symbol was wrong, even though it was a transgender symbol. She remembered now seeing another symbol used sometimes, especially for intersex people, hermaphrodites. It was a circle with the same cross beneath and horns above, a mix of the signs of Venus and Mercury.

Venus and Mercury, these were the parents of the original hermaphrodite, Hermes and Aphrodite to the Greeks. He was literally a mix of these two. But the symbol in blood had not been Venus and Mercury. It had been Venus and Mars. Venus and Mars had had children too, not nearly so romantic as Hermaphroditus. No, the mix of Venus and Mars would symbolise something far more fearful...

Two men stood inside Jane Cavendish's living room, silent and unmoving, just waiting for her. She gasped in shock and her whole mind lost its focus instantaneously. Her horn rimmed spectacles remained in the bathroom. Without them, she could only just focus on the looming, threatening figures as they stepped towards her. Even so, she could be in no doubt that these tall, wiry, bald men were just the same ones that had attacked Saphy in London.

Out in the open, in the park, with the surprise assistance of her unlikely companion, Saphy had managed to escape them. Here, in the confined space of her living room, unaided and with no help likely to appear, Jane did not feel so confident. In fact, just looking at these two men as they drew out a pair of angry looking daggers, had her rooted to the spot with fear. Even if she wanted to try and run now, her legs just would not do it.

There was something about these men, their presence, the way they looked at her and moved, that caused terror to run right down her spine. Her limbs just turned to jelly. The towel held up by her arms dropped to the ground, leaving her body naked and revealed. That very nakedness that had seemed so right and natural when she was alone in the shower, now served to do nothing but make her feel horribly exposed. Seeing her ripe, sensual body, her breasts and penis together like that, caused both men to make a horrific guttural hissing sound.

"Unnatural beast," one said, advancing on her, "Monstrous creature. We will see that you do not remain among us."

"We will fill your last moments with horror," the other one sneered, a fixed frowning sneer on his face that matched his twin exactly, "Fear and dread!"

"Of course," Jane had a moment of revelation, finally realising what her mind had been reaching for, "The symbol. The spawn of Venus and Mars. Fear and dread. Phobus and Deimus!"

Phobus and Deimus, if that was how they had chosen to style themselves, simply grinned evilly at this. That was their sole method of agreement. They stood over Jane's naked, terror filled body and raised their ugly knives in unison. Jane's head span as the two sharp blades plunged deep into her chest and the blood began to flow. Her final thoughts flew to Saphy, fearful that her former student had got so far in over her head that her fate would soon be the same as Jane's own.

Gabe wandered in soft, green grass, his mind floating far away from the world. Everything here felt more heightened, more vibrant and alive. The soft grass beneath his bare feet, the warm sun beating down on his shoulders, the cool breeze wafting over his naked body, the sound of running, tumbling water; it all felt more real than reality. He never wanted to leave this place. He could just stay walking in this soft green grass forevermore.

He turned towards the sound of falling water. He began to recognise this place. He had expected to see a stream, but instead there was a fountain. It was built like a well, a round stone structure about waist height with a pool of water inside. In the centre of this pool, a jet of water shot up into the air before tumbling and splashing back into the water. Gabe felt an incredible urge to bathe his naked body in the cool, clear waters of the fountain.

As he headed towards the falling water, he saw a figure emerge up out of the pool. It was the figure of a beautiful woman, one that made Gabe's whole body instantly alive with excitement. Her tall, elegant body was completely naked, the waters of the fountain running right down it as she stood there, right in the middle of the fountain. Her hair, a rich golden shade, fell down to her waist and wrapped around her body. Gabe knew her instantly as the goddess that stalked all his finest dreams, Venus the Queen of Love.

"Come, my son," came the wondrous, musical voice, thrumming through every fibre of his being, "Come see what you are. Come look in my mirror."

She reached out her hand to him and Gabe found that he too was now standing inside the water as it splashed against his naked skin. He too stretched out his hand to touch hers so he was posed in an exact mirror image of the goddess. As his fingers touched hers, he felt a feeling like a burst of electricity exploding right through his body, from the tips of his fingers right down to his toes. He felt alive and throbbing with need. His body felt so soft and sensitive and yet, beneath the water line, he could feel all the blood rushing to his growing erection.

The goddess' perfect lips drew themselves into a smile. Red lips and bright white teeth conveying all kinds of depths of warmth, love and desire that made Gabe feel pretty light headed. He felt himself smiling back, his own movements almost involuntarily following hers. As she moved her hand from where it touched his, his own hand followed suit. She reached up and ran her hands through her golden hair where the shower of water fell on her head. Gabe copied and ran his hands through his darker locks, finding them seeming to grow longer with his touch.

Looking into the falling water, Gabe could see that the image of Venus before him was no longer the golden haired goddess he knew. She had darker hair, although the beautiful soft, pale skin and the curves of her breasts were still the same. Her face was now partly obscured by the water falling on her. Gabe reached out to touch her once more, but his hand passed right through the water without grasping anything. He realised that he was no longer looking at the goddess, but a reflection in the running water. He was looking at himself.

He looked down at his body. It was the usual awkward, skinny shape he was used to, the one that made him feel uncomfortable about himself. The image he saw in the mirror, however, was a different kind of him, one with a beautiful body, a soft, sensual, curvy form. He could feel an incredible yearning for the body in the reflection. He knew it was him and yet not him and he longed to change that, to feel as beautiful as she looked.

He reached out, trying to touch that soft skin, but all he got was wetness. Touching the face of his reflection just served to disrupt the cherished image. As he passed his hand through the indistinct face, it began to change again. The hair that had been blonde and was now a dark brown was beginning to turn a new shade. It was beginning to turn purple. It flickered purple for a moment, then shifted again to blonde, then bright red.

The woman in the water seemed to shift right through a rainbow of colours, red one minute, green the next. Gabe did not really understand what was happening in this transformation, but he remained fascinated, excited and rooted to the spot. The woman who had seemed his reflection until a few seconds ago now stepped forward naked from the shower of water. Her hair turned back to purple. It was Saphy.

This was not what Gabe expected at all. He was lost in the paradise pleasure of his dream world with his beautiful goddess, imagining himself far more comfortable in his nakedness than he could ever be in reality, then that dream world was invaded by the image of that frustrating, angry, aggressive girl. Still, he could not take his eyes off hers. Beneath the row of glittering piercings along Saphy's eyebrows, Gabe had never before noticed the bright green of her eyes.

"Gabe," she said, pushily, "Get up."

And then she seemed to burst into bubbles. One minute Saphy was standing there in the fountain before the naked Gabe, the next she was splashing water everywhere and had completely disappeared. The splash hit Gabe hard in the face, soaking him wet and bringing him to his senses.

He woke up slumped on a hard wood floor. His head ached worse than he could ever remember it and his eyes struggled to focus around him. It slowly dawned on him that he was still alive, much to his surprise. He was not dead, nor was he lost in a fantasy world. He would never feel this groggy if he were dead. Something, some kind of good fortune, had preserved him when he thought all was lost. All he remembered was the two sinister twins sticking a knife against his back and then he had felt a terrible pain in his head and he had blacked out. Now he woke up here.

After a few moments' effort to focus his attention, Gabe looked around the room where he found himself. It was a bare, empty room in some kind of basement or cellar. The walls were unpainted plaster and the floor wood. There were bars like a cage or a prison, behind which Gabe was shut.

From behind a door in the bars a man dressed in a sort of robe or cowl watched Gabe. He had a bucket of water, which he had just poured over Gabe to wake him. Beneath the hood of the cowl, the man was simply watching in silence. The robe he wore was black, but there was a design on it. It was a white shape, like a cross but growing from narrow points in the middle to a wide end on each of the cross' four edges. Gabe was not thinking very clearly at this point, but he felt frustrated to have understood one mysterious symbol only to be confronted with another.

He was about to open his dry mouth to ask the silent watcher some question, when the robed man turned and walked out of the room. Gabe could hear his footsteps going upstairs. He began to wonder what he had been brought here for. Why would they keep him alive? What were they going to do to him now in this dungeon? He slumped on the floor in despair, finding himself incapable of trying to figure out the whole situation.

As time went by and nothing happened, Gabe began to think a little clearer. He could no longer hear the footsteps anywhere in the building. Finally, he got up and walked around his small cell. Knowing full well that nothing would happen he leaned with the full force of his weight against the door. To his surprise, the door opened instantly, nearly throwing Gabe back down to the floor.

Not wasting any time considering why the door was left unlocked, Gabe ran across the room and up the stairs. He could still hear no noises in the house, but he wasn't taking any chances on checking the place out. Seeing the front door he headed straight out onto the street and started to run. He had no idea which way he was running or where to, he just knew he wanted to get away from there.

Running full tilt down the unfamiliar streets of Cambridge, with no idea of where he was in the city, Gabe almost ran headlong into a street sign. Looking up he saw it pointed in the direction of the railway station. Right then he knew that after his experience he wanted to put Cambridge as far behind him as possible. He remembered Saphy saying she would wait there for him until seven and then leave. He checked his watch. It was

6:55. Glancing up at the sign, he followed the direction it lead and broke once more into a run as fast as he could.

Seven o'clock had just passed when Gabe turned onto the street with the station on it. There was no sign of Saphy waiting outside. Gabe was severely out of breath, his body beginning to ache from all the running and his head throbbing with the pain of where he had been knocked out, but he had to keep running. He had to get away. He could not risk being caught again. After a moment to catch his breath, he broke into a run once more.

With his head down, he ran straight into the chest of a man who stood right over him. He felt strong arms grab him by the shoulders and panic ran right down his spine once more. He looked up in fear, preparing himself for the sight of the two bald assassins he had tussled with twice already. Instead, he found himself looking into the frowning, hard face of a policeman.

"You're in an awful hurry, sunshine," he said, "Running from something in particular?"

Gabe sat at a desk in a police interrogation room, feeling truly dreadful. He felt tired and confused and the pain in his head just would not go away. The way the police had treated his rambling account of the day's events hadn't especially helped his mood. Unsurprisingly, they had reacted just as Saphy had predicted to the suggestion that anybody was killed because a four hundred year old painting of a woman was maybe a man. They were equally easy to convince of the idea that Gabe had been assaulted, kidnapped and locked in a basement for the past couple of hours, a basement he could not properly describe nor locate. He had to admit that the whole thing sounded pretty far fetched even to him, and he had lived it.

The door of the interrogation room opened and two police officers entered. One was the one that had already interviewed Gabe for an hour, seeming not to believe a single word of his story. He was a tough looking, broad shouldered man with a military haircut and a condescending attitude. The other man was obviously the first policeman's superior. He was of a slighter build, while still being bigger and stronger than Gabe, but carried himself with an air of efficient command.

"I'm Detective Inspector Gilbert," he introduced himself, "And you've already met Detective Sergeant Godfrey. We'd like to ask you a few questions." "I've already told him everything that's happened," Gabe said, sounding frustrated and petulant but mostly exhausted after the day he had had.

"Now then, there's no need for you to take that tone with us, Mr. Herrison," DI Gilbert went on, "We're just trying to establish exactly what happened this afternoon. Can you tell us again where you were between the hours of five and seven?"

"I was locked in a basement somewhere in town," Gabe said, "I was attacked, assaulted in the street by a couple of robed assassins and when I woke up I was in this cellar."

"Locked in a basement by a sinister cult? That's your story, Mr. Herrison?" DI Gilbert seemed disbelieving, "A locked basement that you just walked out of when the time came for you to leave. A locked basement that you can't tell us even roughly the whereabouts of. I'm sorry, Mr. Herrison, but I'm having a little trouble believing this story. I think you have a very fertile imagination, right Godfrey?" "Right, sir. Very fertile," DS Godfrey agreed, eyeing Gabe up in a threatening fashion.

"What about before that then, Mr. Herrison," DI Gilbert continued, "You gave us a London address, so what are you doing here in Cambridge?"

"I came to the university, to see a professor," Gabe explained, "Jane Cavendish. I needed her help with something."

"Needed her help?" Gilbert repeated, giving his colleague a significant glance as he said this, "Was it perhaps in connection with this?"

He opened the file that he was carrying and placed a glossy A4 size photograph on the table between Gabe and the two detectives. Gabe recognised it instantly. It showed the victim of the National Gallery murder, the middle aged woman in a white smock, stretched out on the floor, blood leaking from her neck, the now familiar symbol drawn onto the wall. It was an image that Gabe needed no photo to remember, it was embedded in his mind for good.

"Recognise that?" Gilbert went on.

"I took it," Gabe agreed, "On the day of the murder in the National Gallery. I turned all my photos over to the Metropolitan Police."

"So, you were there with the victim on the day of that murder," Gilbert responded, flashing another significant glance at Godfrey, "None of your photos give any indication of the perpetrator of this heinous crime," the tone he used as he said this had a whiff of sarcasm that Gabe could not quite follow, "Just gruesome images of the victim, right, Godfrey?"

"Right, sir," Godfrey agreed again, "Nothing but shots of a dying body. Never stepped in to lend a hand."

"What can you tell us about this?" Gilbert pointed to the symbol drawn in blood on the wall.

"It's a transgender symbol," Gabe replied, pleased to be able to use the knowledge he'd recently gained.

"So, it means that somebody's a tranny," Gilbert repeated, "A man who wants to be a girl?"

"A she-male," Godfrey agreed, leeringly, "A chick with a dick."

"And this is the reason you came to see Professor Cavendish?" DI Gilbert asked.

"Exactly," Gabe agreed with a sigh of relief, finally feeling that the detectives were beginning to piece things together properly.

"So, in your expert opinion, what do you make of this?" Gilbert's tone continued to have that uncomfortable note of sarcasm in it, "The same thing?"

"Looks like the same to me, sir," Godfrey agreed.

Gilbert took another glossy photo from his file and placed it down on the desk. Gabe leaned over to look at it. The photo showed the head and torso of a grey haired woman. She was naked with her breasts exposed. The blank expression in her eyes showed Gabe that the woman was dead, but he took a few moments to register that the naked dead woman was Professor Cavendish, the same woman who he had talked with just a few hours earlier.

CHAPTER 4

The throbbing ache in his head seemed to get worse. He couldn't breathe for a moment. His head spun and he felt almost as if he was about to faint. There was a sick feeling building up in the pit of his stomach. Struggling to focus his eyes on the photo, all he could see for a moment was grey. The pain in his head made it difficult to think straight. He was struggling to comprehend that in the few short hours since he had talked with her, the professor could have been brutally murdered.

Looking further at the picture, beginning to focus properly, Gabe could see that her naked body had been nastily mutilated. There were a series of ugly, deep cuts into her chest. After a moment, Gabe realised what he was looking at amongst the blood and gore. The cuts formed a circle with a cross beneath and an arrow coming from the top right. It was the image that he was beginning to see everywhere, that symbol he had never seen before this last week but knew so well now. The transgender sign.

"Yes," Gabe admitted, when he could finally bring himself to speak, "That looks like the same symbol. Do you think we're dealing with a serial killer? Might I be the next target? Why didn't they kill me already?"

"It certainly seems likely that there's a link between the two killings," DI Gilbert confirmed, "It seems too much of a coincidence to see two such victims in such close succession with this same symbol attached to each."

"Two such victims?" Gabe asked, confused.

"Both trannies," Gilbert responded, "Right, Godfrey?"

"Right, sir," his colleague agreed, "Evidence points to a classic case of a hate crime."

"Wait," Gabe cut in, confused and messed up in the head, struggling to keep track of the conversation, "Professor Cavendish was transgender?"

He guessed that should not really surprise him given her field of study. Then it hit him, the bigger revelation in that sentence, something he really should have picked up on before.

"And...And the first victim?" he gasped, suddenly putting things together, "She was one too?"

"Don't play dumb," Godfrey cut in, aggressively, "Of course she bloody was. You just told us what the symbol meant, remember!"

"I didn't think she was referring to herself," Gabe protested, sounding unconvincing even to himself, "I thought she meant the painting."

"Right," Gilbert sounded unconvinced, "All I'm saying is that you might interpret the appearance of this symbol at both crime scenes as some kind of a link between them. Now, you, Mr. Herrison, had never met either of these, er, for want of a better word, women before?"

"No, never," Gabe said.

"And yet you were the last person to see either of them alive," Gilbert went on, "And you were the one who knew the symbolism of the blood signs at both crime scenes, the one that drew the link between them."

"Why don't you think about that when you tell us where it is you've been all afternoon?" Godfrey added.

"Wait, are you trying to tell me that I'm a suspect?!" Gabe finally managed to get his mind running clearly enough to realise where this conversation had been heading all along.

"No, we're just saying that you're a valuable witness," DI Gilbert replied with a patronising sneer that suggested the truth was more than his words, "One that can help us greatly in our enquiries."

"And we'll be very interested in questioning you further," Godfrey added, "So, I would stick around. Don't be doing anything stupid like leaving the country."

Finally, after being grilled for what seemed like hours, Gabe was able to leave the station. He felt drained and exhausted, both physically and emotionally, his head still throbbed with a pain that made it hard to concentrate on anything else. He just wanted to lie down and sleep and try and block out the memory of what he had seen in those pictures, what had happened to the woman he was talking to just hours earlier.

These were the thoughts running through his mind as he made his way through the police station, already contemplating a soft bed and a pillow for his aching head. Outside, it had been dark for some time. He checked his watch. 10:20. Saphy had left three hours earlier, along with any chance he had at figuring out what had really gone on that afternoon. Just as he thought this, he felt a hand grab his arm for the third time that day.

Gabe couldn't believe his luck. How did this keep happening? Maybe he should pay a little more attention to where he was going and his surroundings, he thought. He felt his heart sink in the knowledge that some new trouble was about to be heaped onto his shoulders. Feeling light headed all of a sudden, he was about to faint to the floor when he looked up at the arm holding onto his and the person behind him. It was Saphy.

"Come on," she said, her upper class accent bringing Gabe back round to focus on reality, "We're getting out of here."

As a child, the idea of getting a train from London to Paris through a tunnel under the sea seemed wondrous and exciting to Gabe. It seemed like the sort of thing that would only happen in a fantastical story and yet it had happened, the tunnel had been built and now here he found himself on the train travelling to the City of Lights beside a woman who was nearly a perfect stranger to him.

The day before, Gabe had been specifically told by the police not to leave the country and now he found himself doing just that. When he had told Saphy, as they travelled back from Cambridge to London, the story of everything that had happened to him that afternoon and what the police had told him the day before, she had said that that was just why they had to leave the country and do it as soon as possible.

"If they're telling you not to leave the country now, that means that in a couple of days there'll probably get around to blocking your passport," Saphy had said, "If we ever want to solve this mystery we need to leave now before they stop us."

"Why do we have to leave the country?" Gabe had wondered.

"Well, for one, if the police are after you as their prime suspect, it's probably best to get as far from them as possible," Saphy replied, "For another, if we really think that following the clues and searching for the Fountain of Salmacis is the way to find out just what is happening here, then we'll have to go abroad. I seriously doubt we can find the fountain in Britain. Thirdly, if the police made a point of telling you not to leave the country, I suspect they have some vested interest in keeping you here beyond you being a suspect."

"What do you mean?" Gabe asked.

"How do you think you were able to escape from that cellar? Why weren't you as brutally butchered as Jane?" Saphy demanded, quite aggressively, almost as if she blamed him for not dying instead of her former mentor, "They let you escape, Gabe, they wanted you to get away and get caught. How do you think that the police were able to pick you up so quickly and have all their evidence to hand if they weren't directed that way?"

"I don't understand, you think it was a setup?" Gabe responded.

"Yeah, I think that whoever these people are, they're powerful enough to have some kind of hold over the police," Saphy agreed, "But not powerful enough to make a dead body just completely disappear. The murder at the gallery was on the front page of all the national papers and got loads of TV coverage. The police can't just let the case lie. They need to be seen to be investigating it. They need a suspect, a fall guy. Today they were able to engineer a situation in which you could be that fall guy. It ties up all their loose ends, gets you and Jane out of the way."

"And what about you?" Gabe had asked, feeling perhaps a little suspicious over how Saphy had remained unharmed throughout all of this.

"I didn't provide any witness statements or anything for the London murder," Saphy reminded him, "And I had an alibi for this afternoon. I was at the library surrounded by people, not locked in some mystery basement. I'm sure that once they have the time to pick over the evidence and your photos properly, they'll want to question me further. Something that I have no interest in. I've dealt with the police before, enough to not have a lot of faith in them. That's why we have to leave before they catch up with us."

"So, where are we going then?" Gabe had asked, "What are we looking for? It is definitely 'we' now then?"

"Like you said before, we're in this together whether we like it or not," Saphy replied, "I think we're both agreed that the sooner we figure out the mystery, the sooner we can present a real suspect and clear out names."

"Right," Gabe agreed, "And the best way to do that is to follow the clues that we have, to seek out the secrets in the Rokeby Venus and see if it leads us to Salmacis."

"Exactly," Saphy agreed, "Glad to see that we are on the same wavelength at last. While I was in the library, I looked up everything that I could about the Hermaphroditus legend and the Borghese Hermaphroditus. I never want to take something a professor says at face value, I want to have it confirmed by my own researches. What did you find out from Dr. Gerard?"

"I'm pretty sure that Robert White was looking for the Fountain of Salmacis when he disappeared," Gabe responded, excitedly, "I found this on his desk. I can't make sense especially of the list, but it shows he was interested in the Borghese sculpture."

Gabe fished around in his pocket and pulled out a crumpled piece of paper. He unfolded it and placed it on the table in front of them. The black and white image of the Hermaphroditus sculpture was visible despite being pretty poor quality. Saphy looked down the list of place names, looking quite pleased with the discovery.

"The Louvre, Uffizi, the Met, they're all major museums," she said, "The museums and collections that have a copy of the sculpture. Like Jane said, the Borghese sculpture is not the original, it's just the first copy to be rediscovered. All these other museums have versions as well, either Roman copies like the Borghese one or later copies of that. The copy Velazquez had made is in the Prado in Madrid. Not only does this prove that White was interested in the sculpture, it gives us a course to follow. If White thought he could find out about the Fountain of Salmacis through looking at these sculptures then we'd do well to follow."

"But, which one?" Gabe asked.

"I'd say we could do plenty worse than start at the beginning," Saphy said, looking at the first name on the list, "The first version of the sculpture, the one that used to be on display in the Villa Borghese, is now on display in Paris, in the Louvre. If we leave London first thing tomorrow, Paris is the first place we can get to. We can be there by lunchtime."

That was how Gabe now found himself on board a train speeding beneath the English Channel, heading for Paris and more mysteries locked in classical works of art. He had not managed to get much sleep the night before, returning late to his flat and having to pack up a case for this morning's trip and then get up before sunrise to get to the station. He felt tired and a little grumpy and the pain in his head from being knocked out the day before was still feeling pretty sore.

"You know this mystery is thousands of years old," he complained, "I'm sure it could have waited a few more hours to be solved. Then we could have actually got a little sleep."

"Not been getting your beauty sleep, pretty boy?" Saphy teased, "That wouldn't please your vain goddess."

"Hmph," Gabe made a sulky noise, "My goddess? You're the one with her symbol inked into your skin."

"OK, OK," Saphy laughed, "That reminds me, I picked up a little something in the library you might like."

She opened her bag and pulled out a book. Gabe's heart skipped a beat as he took in the faded and torn cover, the golden haired goddess rising from the sea. It was Love's Children. His own copy had been lost years ago, when he was still a child. For a couple of years he had looked for the book whenever in a book shop but with little luck. After a while he had just given up and started to forget about it, right up until the events of the past week had thrown Venus and the legend of Hermaphroditus violently back into his thoughts. And now he had found it again, the book that had meant so much to him, now he could hold it in his hands, turn the pages and read the story he had once known by heart.

"Oh, thank you," Gabe said excitedly, genuinely thrilled to have the book in his possession once more, "This is amazing."

"It's just a book," Saphy responded, offhand, "And not a very popular one at that."

"That's what makes it so special," Gabe replied, "It's the best present I've had in years."

"Which is kind of tragic, when you put it like that," she said, "You've not had anything better than an ageing library book in all that time?"

"If it's a library book, won't somebody mind that you're taking it away?" he asked.

"It's sort of on a permanent loan."

"You mean you stole it?" he said, slightly aghast.

"I prefer to think of it as liberating the book, redistributing it where it will be better appreciated," she said, pouting a little like a sulky child, "Look, I thought you were pleased, but if you don't want to be accepting stolen goods I'll just have it back."

She snatched the book back off him, causing the flimsy cover to rip a little further. He blushed red with either embarrassment or irritation, it was hard to tell, and grabbed it back from her.

"No, I'll keep it," he said decisively, but the moment between them was gone, her touching gesture of finding the book that meant more to him than she really knew, and his genuine gratitude was buried beneath his shyness and her prickly temperament.

They sat there alongside each other, staring blankly forwards at the seatbacks in front of them as the darkness of the tunnel flashed by outside the window. Gabe flicked idly through the pages of the book, not really taking in the stories of Hymenaeus, disguised as a woman to follow his beloved, and Priapus, cursed with a giant penis and driven constantly by lust and impotence, as he ran backwards through the yellowing leaves of the 1970s publication. On the inside cover was a picture of the author, Robert White, as a young man not much older than Gabe himself. There was something about those high cheekbones and narrow, pointed jaw line that seemed familiar to Gabe, but whether it was just a reminder of the hours spent staring at this book as a child he could not tell.

As he randomly turned the pages through Dido burning herself alive on a funeral pyre to her spirit's snub of her former lover in the underworld, Gabe's mind wandered onto the woman sitting beside him. He could see how she had managed to push people away all her life; that was obviously what had happened between her and her former mentor, Professor Cavendish. He found himself getting annoyed at how Saphy would react whenever there was a moment when she let her guard down, she would become aggressive in the next instant.

Finally, admitting he obviously could not concentrate on the book, he got his bag out and slid the book into it. Unfortunately for him, this action just attracted Saphy's attention and gave her a new outlet for her sulky annoyance.

"Didn't I tell you to pack light?" she said, "We don't want to be tied down anywhere. Why did you have to bring all that stuff?"

"You just can't bear to spend any time settled anywhere, can you?" Gabe demanded, annoyed at her always taking the confrontational position, "Can you ever just be in one place that makes you happy or do you need to be always running and fighting?"

"In case you don't remember, we're running because we're being chased," Saphy replied with her voice raised so that other passengers on the train started looking round, "It's not like we had a choice other than stick around and end up butchered like Jane! So, as we're likely to be doing quite a bit of running, couldn't you have brought a bit less stuff? What the hell have you got in those bags, anyway?"

"It's all my camera equipment," Gabe explained, a little embarrassed, opening his bag and pulling out various black lumpy objects, "Wide angle lens, telephoto, macro lens for close ups," he listed the objects as he pulled them out, "Tripod, remote control, underwater housing."

"Underwater housing?" Saphy asked, as if offended by the very idea, taking and examining the object, a grey box the shape of the camera that went around the outside of the whole thing, completely encasing the camera to make it waterproof, "You planning on taking a deep sea diving trip while we're trying to solve this murder mystery?"

"It doesn't hurt to be prepared," Gabe answered sulkily, "It makes me feel better to have all this stuff with me just in case I need it."

"If you're going to bring a bloody comfort blanket, next time make it something a little lighter," she responded.

"Well, it's this comfort blanket that allowed us to figure out the first clue," Gabe was really getting annoyed after that last jibe, "I'd never have seen the symbol or found you otherwise, and then we'd never know anything about it."

"And we'd never have gone to Cambridge and seen Jane," Saphy added, "And she'd probably still be alive. That's where your comfort camera has got us. You've got an innocent woman killed. A woman who never did anything but try and teach and support people on their way in the world!"

Gabe had no comeback for this and, fortunately for him, he did not try to come up with one. A part of him felt that maybe Saphy was right, that he should feel guilt for Professor Cavendish's death, that he had blood on his hands. Equally, he began to understand how shaken up Saphy was by it, how much she had valued Professor Cavendish as a friend and mentor.

Nobody close to Gabe had ever died, he did not have enough people close to him for that to be that likely, so he knew he had no real words of comfort to offer her. He knew, equally, that she would be in no mood to accept any comfort he might tentatively offer and he had no desire to be on the end of another angry tirade. So, they once more sat in silence until they got into France and a customs official had to check their passports.

As they handed the documents over, Gabe felt panic rising up inside him. He had tried to block the thought out all through the journey, but he was starting to wonder now whether the police might really have told customs officials not to take his passport, not to let him into their country. He was, after all, a murder suspect, he told himself. That wave of fear grew bigger and bigger as the official spent significantly longer looking at his and Saphy's passports than he had any of the other passengers'. Finally he turned to Gabe and held up one of the passports.

"Is this you?" he questioned.

Gabe looked at the document in his hand and didn't know whether to laugh or be offended. The picture showed a pretty teenage girl. She was probably about fifteen or sixteen with smooth, straight shoulder length brown hair and soft smooth skin, dressed in a conservative looking blouse and with a rather sweet smile. Even though the printed letters beside the photograph read "Persephone Cross", Gabe was having a little trouble reconciling the girl in the picture with the prickly punk beside him. Obviously the passport inspector was having a similar trouble.

"No it bloody well isn't," Saphy came in, as ever when talking to anyone official her naturally upper-class accent became more pronounced and commanding, "Does he look like a girl to you?"

"I think he's more thinking that she doesn't look any more like you than she does me," Gabe pointed to the photo, smirking.

Finally, the official returned their passports and Gabe was able to relax. In fact, the sight of a totally different Saphy in her passport photo had made him feel quite a lot better, although it had done little to improve her mood.

"Don't ever mention this again," she hissed angrily, after the official had moved onto the next people.

"I just can't believe you ever looked like that," Gabe smiled.

The Palace of the Louvre is a grand and imposing building. The former official residence of France's royal family, there are parts of the building from almost every century in the last five hundred years. Most recently, in the last thirty years, a great pyramid has been constructed from 673 panes of glass right in the centre between the building's wings. This piece of perfect modernist beauty wonderfully offsets the 17th century architecture behind it. It is a sight that greats increasingly many visitors from far and wide, all of whom travel beneath the glass pyramid to witness one of the finest art collections in the world.

Many are drawn to the museum's famous paintings, hoping that they will be the one to decode the mysteries of the Mona Lisa's famous smile. Gabe and Saphy, however, had their minds on a different mystery when they passed beneath the Louvre pyramid in search of the museum's incredible displays of classical sculpture.

Upstairs, a huge crowd was gathered around a statue, tall, elegant and beautiful, a woman with her pointed breasts bared. The cloth draping over her body seemed to be caught just at the moment when it slipped from her, with part of her buttocks tantalisingly exposed. Her left arm was missing from the shoulder and her right arm from just above the elbow, but otherwise she was perfect.

"The Venus de Milo," Saphy explained, "For the last two hundred years, she's been the most famous image of our goddess in classical art."

Her mingled grief and anger had abated somewhat since they were on the train. The incident with her passport photo, much as it had brought out her aggressive side, had served to distract her from the much more serious issues on her mind and she had gradually lightened up as they got closer to Paris. On entering the museum, Saphy seemed in her element. Gabe watched impressed as she appreciated the beautiful statues and sculptures of gods and mythical figures, of all of whom she knew the story.

"Come on," she said, "We need to be downstairs."

She walked ahead with purpose, leaving Gabe with little choice but to follow her lead. She seemed to know better than him where to go and what to do. He had to admit that he liked seeing this side to her, only briefly glimpsed before in the cab to Cambridge and Professor Cavendish's office. Gabe was beginning to see how

much Saphy enjoyed being amongst beautiful art and being able to understand and explain it. He saw how she appreciated his presence at those times. Even while she was conveying how uninformed she found him, she appeared to enjoy being the one to inform him.

She led Gabe into a long white room filled with antique sculpture. The walls were lined with columns that grew to form a row of arches along the ceiling. At the far end, four tall female figures stood two on either side of a doorway. White marble figures stood on a red and white diamond patterned floor, giving the whole place a sort of ghostly feel. As they walked between the figures, Gabe could not help feeling an eerie sense as if they had all been real people turned to stone by a vengeful woman cursed by the gods.

As they walked down the room toward the four giant figures at the opposite end, Gabe studied the statues they passed. Many of them showed Venus, the goddess that always lurked at the back of his mind. There she was crouched on her knees, her arm covering her breasts almost protectively and here she was turned away, as if somewhat bashful, grasping her drapery around her topless body. Another goddess stood proudly in the middle of the room, one hand resting on a stag, the other pulling an arrow from the quiver on her back. Seeing that arrow was an unpleasant reminder for Gabe of what he had witnessed the last time he was in a museum, but he tried to push the thought away.

Then he saw it. Watched over by the four imposing figures around the door, lounging on a mattress that looked so textured that Gabe would have been surprised to touch the marble and not find it as soft as lamb's wool, was Hermaphroditus. He had seen the photo in Professor Cavendish's book, but it did not do justice to the beauty of the figure, the curve of his hip, the soft round flesh of his buttocks, and that little penis nestled between the feminine body and the soft mattress. Gabe could well see how this image had captivated minds four hundred years earlier. His arms were folded on the soft pillow and his serene face looked out from there, just as it looked out from the mirror in Velazquez's painting.

"Wow," Gabe said, and then, after a moment, thinking back to the words Saphy had said when they had been back in Cambridge, "How did that poem go?"

"'Lift up thy lips, turn round, look back for love,
Blind love that comes by night and casts out rest;
Of all things tired thy lips look weariest,
Save the long smile that they are wearied of.
Ah sweet, albeit no love be sweet enough,
Choose of two loves and cleave unto the best;
Two loves at either blossom of thy breast
Strive until one be under and one above.'" Saphy quoted, "It's a very tragic poem really. It's all about the impossibility of someone so lovely and yet neither man nor woman ever finding love when men only desire women and women, men. He is something strange, wonderful and unique."

"Not completely unique, though," Gabe said, "Surely the waters of the fountain could have turned others into creatures like him."

"I don't know what you're thinking we're going to discover, Gabe, but I think it's pretty unlikely, if not impossible, that there actually are waters that can turn a man feminine," Saphy replied.

"But, surely if all these people are desperate to discover the fountain, if they're willing to kill for it...?" Gabe asked, leaving the end of his question hanging.

"That just means that they believe it, not that it's true," Saphy told him, "Think of all the wars that have been fought over religion. They can't all be right and yet they're all willing to kill for what they believe. Look, I just want to find whatever it is that they're looking for so we can uncover just what is behind these murders. I don't expect to witness some kind of supernatural wonders."

"Right," Gabe agreed, but his heart sank a little at her very rational argument, telling him that he had raised his hopes unreasonably, "So, I guess we need to examine the sculpture. How are we going to do that?"

There was a barrier running around the statue that prevented the two of them from getting up close enough to examine it properly. Looking around, Gabe noticed that they were being watched not only by the four female statues beside the door, but by a flesh and blood guard, wandering between the statues, eyeing up anyone who looked a little suspicious until they turned and walked away.

"We're never going to be able to look closely with him around," Gabe said.

"Don't worry, I've got an idea," Saphy said.

Gabe stood beside the statue as he watched the girl with the bright purple hair, standing out as an anomaly amongst the white marble statues even more than she had in the National Gallery in London, as she walked straight over and started talking to the guard in rapid and expressive French. Gabe had not realised that his companion knew the language at all, but she was clearly managing to speak pretty fluently and being completely understood by the guard. Saphy was pointing to him a lot and both looked over at one point to see Gabe smiling back awkwardly.

After a few minutes of this, they both came over towards Gabe. The guard's previously frowning expression was a happier one now. He shook Gabe by the hand in a surprisingly friendly fashion and then drew the barrier aside to allow Gabe and Saphy through to see the Hermaphroditus up close. Gabe took out his camera and began to photograph the statue, looking over it for any signs of something out of the ordinary. While he did this, he carried out a conversation with Saphy in hushed whispers.

"What did you say to him?" he asked.

"I told him that you were Professor Robert White from Cambridge University and I was your translator," Saphy smirked, "And that you had come to examine the Hermaphroditus as part of your research." "Why am I the professor?" Gabe asked, "Surely if he has any questions then you're then one with all the knowledge."

"Do I look like a professor?" she replied, "And anyway, it doesn't matter what you say to me in English,

I'll just translate it into my own brilliant ideas in French!"

"And he accepted me as Robert White? And that I'd be here without any other authorisation?"

"Well, we know that White has obviously been here before, so I figured the name would be familiar to him," Saphy explained, "This building is so vast that you could easily have not managed to find your way to the right place to report yourself and who you were visiting, that must happen with academic visitors quite often. Besides, I told him that Louis Philippe had allowed it."

"Who?"

"The curator," Saphy explained.

"How do you know that?"

"I looked it up before we left. I thought it was the kind of knowledge that might prove useful. You can get into most places in life just by seeming to know what you're doing, having a confident attitude and knowing the name of someone on the inside," she told him, impressing Gabe with her level of sneaky forethought, "Now, as long as you don't do anything stupid and continue to behave like a professor studying the statue, he shouldn't suspect anything. It's more than his job's worth to bother stopping us if we don't mess with the statue at all."

For the next two hours, Gabe and Saphy studied the statue closely from every angle, exploring, examining and photographing every inch of the marble curves, looking for any imperfections, any slight signs that could set them off onto their next clue. All this searching, however, was in vain. The statue was perfect. There was nothing about it to suggest anything more than could be seen on the surface. Finally, they had to admit defeat. If there was anything special about this statue, it was not something that the two of them could find.

"Let's find a hotel," Saphy suggested at last, "We're going to have to re-think our plans. There's six more museums on White's list, I guess we're going to have to think which of them will be our next best option."

As they were leaving the gallery, Saphy decided she needed to use the bathroom, no great surprise after spending a couple of hours studying the statue, and told Gabe to wait for her there. Gabe stood amongst the blank eyes of the marble statues, feeling uncomfortably like he was being watched. Out of the corner of his eye he saw a flash of white material and suddenly was reminded once more of the day of the first murder. He had been convinced that he had seen a similar wisp of material rapidly disappearing a moment after the arrow struck the unfortunate victim. He had seen nothing to confirm that impression in any of his photos and had gradually forgotten ever seeing it. Now, however, all those impressions came flooding back.

He looked anxiously around. He was all alone. Even the guard was nowhere to be seen. There was nothing but antique statues, gods, goddesses and heroes all stuck in complete stillness. Only, something was wrong, something was different. There was a figure he had not noticed before. He looked towards the statue of the huntress with a deer and a quiver full of arrows and saw a similar woman beside her. She was also dressed in a simple white tunic, carrying a quiver full of arrows. In her hand she had a bow, however, drawn with one of the arrows on the string, pointed straight at Gabe. It took Gabe this moment to realise why she looked wrong. This was no marble statue but a flesh and blood woman, standing as still as a statue but with peachy skin and jet black curls of hair.

"Do not seek our fallen sister," the archer woman said in heavily accented English, still pointing her arrow directly at Gabe's heart. He could see the white feathers of the arrow's fletching were just the same as the ones he had seen sticking out of the dead woman's neck a few days before.

"What?" he asked, "I don't understand." "I am Atalanta, a naiad of Diana, and I come to warn you," the strange woman replied, "Do not seek for the secret of Salmacis. I and my sisters are the guardians of this secret, sworn to keep Salmacis' shame from the world. If you attempt to discover and to reveal Salmacis' shame then the naiads will silence you as we have done since time immemorial."

At that moment, Gabe heard other footsteps coming into the gallery. He turned his head to see the unmistakable shock of purple hair that told him Saphy was on her way over. He turned back to Atalanta, so many questions still on the end of his tongue, and saw nothing but the statue of the huntress and the deer. Once again, as in the National Gallery, all he could see was a wisp of white fabric, fluttering quickly out of view.

ENCHANTED SOUL PART 2

CHAPTER 1

"Diana was the goddess of the moon and of the hunt," Saphy explained to Gabe after they had checked into a local hotel and Gabe had told her of his strange encounter back at the Louvre, "She was noted as the virgin goddess. After talking to Jane, I read Francis Beaumont's poem, Salmacis and Hermaphroditus. Beaumont says that the young Hermaphroditus was so beautiful that he tempted even the virginal Diana into lustful thoughts. The naiads were followers of Diana, they were water spirits as devoted to virginity and purity as she was."

"But, wasn't Salmacis a water spirit?" Gabe asked, "Wasn't she a naiad?"

"She was, and a very unusual one in being driven more by lust and the hunt for sex rather than actual hunting," Saphy replied, "That's probably what your

Atalanta meant by describing the fountain as 'Salmacis' shame'. She obviously feels that the cursed waters represent a failure of a naiad to pursue their chosen course of chastity."

"So, doesn't these naiads threatening me suggest that maybe there is some truth to the legend?" Gabe said, excited once more at what they might discover where a few hours earlier Saphy's rational argument had been enough to make him think otherwise.

"Not exactly, no," Saphy replied, "Anybody can call themselves a 'naiad' without having access to any real supernatural secrets or powers. What it does tell us is that there are more people than just our ugly bald friends out to stop us, which, of course, makes me much more determined to find what's going on. It also tells us that these 'naiads' were the ones responsible for the gallery murder and the bald assassins for Jane's death."

"What makes you think that?" Gabe was astounded that Saphy thought she could solve the murders that quickly and rather surprised that this revelation made her actually more determined to solve the ancient mystery of Salmacis.

"Simple," Saphy replied, "Both the naiads and the baldies use pretty distinctive weapons. You've already basically told me that the naiads were responsible for the gallery murder when you told me their arrows were the same. Not many murders with bows and arrows these days, it's a pretty major giveaway. So, I think we can fairly assume, given the symbolic role these arrows play, that they did not murder Jane as she was killed with a knife, and her body butchered, which doesn't seem to fit with the naiads behaviour.

"Those bald guys, however, with their ugly ceremonial dagger and rather narrow moral attitude seem to have just the right weapon for that one, especially as we know from your experience that they were there in Cambridge that day and have some links with the white cross wearing people who locked you in the basement. As far as I can see, both the naiads and the white crosses want to stop information about the fountain slipping out, so both have a vested interest in stopping us. However, the white cross people seem to want to find the fountain for themselves, so the naiads presumably want to stop them too." "So, now we know who the killers are, why don't we just go to the police?" Gabe asked.

"Because, the story is no more plausible now we know more details," Saphy said, "They still wouldn't believe us. We've got no evidence."

"So, we're still going to try and find the fountain?" Gabe asked, fearful both of her saying yes and putting their lives in further jeopardy or no and leaving them with nowhere to turn, leaving the mystery completely uncovered, "Even despite the naiads' threat?"

"Like I said, that just makes me want to know more," Saphy said, putting on a determined and defiant expression, "They want to stop me finding out their secrets. Well, bring it on. I want to know the mystery now as much for the mystery's sake as to save myself. Besides, the naiad's presence at the Louvre gives us two more pieces of information. For one, if they think the statue's worth protecting then it still has some clue to yield up to us. We're going back there tomorrow." "And the other?"

"They obviously know about us," Saphy replied, "They've been able to follow us, observe us and track us down. The white crosses and their creepy assassins are not going to be far behind. We're going to have to be more covert in our actions."

"You're the one that stands out a mile away!" Gabe exclaimed irritably, "Just look at that hair. Of course people can track and follow you."

"Way ahead of you there," Saphy smirked.

To Gabe's surprise she did not get angry or aggressive at his remark, even though that was exactly what he expected her to. Instead, she seemed quite amused at the idea. For the first time since he had met her, Saphy seemed genuinely to be having fun. It was pretty weird fun if the idea of competing against trained assassins and being targeted by mythological virgins was something that made her happy, but Gabe was not about to question the triumphant smile as she went through her luggage and pulled out some scissors and a box of hair dye labelled "Scarlet Passion".

"You know, I think I was going to go redheaded one day anyway," she smiled and headed for the tiny en suite bathroom of their small double room.

"Why did we have to share a room, anyway?" Gabe called through the open bathroom door as he heard the sounds of the snipping of scissors.

"I can't afford any more than that," Saphy responded from the next room, "I don't know how long we'll be chasing around the world solving this mystery and I want to have some money left at the end of it."

"Don't you come from money?" Gabe asked, sure that he had seen plenty of signs of Saphy's expensive education and good breeding beneath her pierced and tattooed exterior.

"Come from is not the same as have now, though, is it?" Saphy responded quite aggressively, peering around the doorway, her hair a half cut mess, brandishing a pair of scissors in a way that was, possibly unintentionally, quite threatening, "I've got a little inheritance from a favourite aunt that I'm now eating through at an alarming rate. After paying for a taxi ride from London to Cambridge and a train from London to Paris, I'm not feeling particularly keen on paying for a plush hotel suite into the bargain."

"Fine. OK," Gabe pacified her, a little concerned about the way she was gesticulating with those scissors, "We'll share a bed then."

"Indiana Jones never had to put up with this," Gabe heard her say to herself under her breath as she ducked back inside the tiny bathroom, "He'd never fail in his quest for the Holy Grail because of bankruptcy."

Gabe found himself smiling in spite of himself at this last muttered remark. Despite her prickly personality, he could not help liking this unusual young woman he had been thrust together with by fate and circumstance.

As the sound of snipping scissors was replaced by running water, Saphy shut the door between bedroom and bathroom, leaving Gabe to his own thoughts. He certainly had a lot to think over given what had happened over the last couple of days, a few mysteries that seemed solved only to present new mysteries in their place. So, the naiads had killed the National Gallery victim, but who was she? Come to that, who were they? Could they really be mythical water spirits protecting their supernatural secret?

All of these mysteries played on Gabe's mind, but he was too tired really to focus on any. His head still ached from the day before and he kept finding himself distracted by the sounds of the shower through the thin wall separating the two rooms. Next door, Saphy was singing. Gabe could hear the muffled sounds of her voice, not the most impressive vocal performance, singing, "You better watch out on what you wish for. It better be worth it, so much to die for."

Of all the mysteries that Gabe was puzzling over, his travelling companion was probably the greatest. Her moods infuriated him, yet he admired the passion with which she believed she was right about virtually everything. He longed to feel that kind of passion about anything, but the only thing that had ever stirred him that way was the story he had once loved to read and re-read. The one in the book that Saphy had given him. The book that she had stolen from the college library. The book that had started another argument between them.

Saphy seemed to wear her heart on her sleeve, quite literally in terms of all her tattoos, and yet Gabe sensed there was more to her than met the eye, more of her story beneath the surface than that which was written on her body. Gabe might not have the strength of tastes and opinions as Saphy did, but he had always prided himself on his ability to read people, to see them through his camera lens and come to some understanding of them. With Saphy, this kind of ability was beyond him and that was beginning to make her a mystery that fascinated him every bit as much as the mythical fountain they were searching for together.

His thoughts were interrupted by their subject exiting the small bathroom wrapped in just a towel. Her hair was now short and spiked up in a completely different style to the neat bob she had sported before. As it dried, the bright red colour of the dye became obvious, every bit as stand out and distinctive as the purple that it had been before. Saphy might have changed her look, but she would still never blend in with the crowd. Maybe she would never be able to suppress that part of her that sought to show off her individuality.

As she sat down on the bed beside him, Gabe couldn't help but notice that the towel barely covered her dripping wet skin. Rivulets of water still ran down her naked skin and Gabe watched it weave between the dark ink of all her body art. He had only seen Saphy before in vests, t-shirts and jackets. Now he discovered there was far more written and drawn across her body than he had thought before. He wondered just what it all meant to her. Just above the level of her towel, he could see the beginning of a quote inked into the small of her back, just below her shoulder blades. It read "Oh mother, dear... "

"What's that?" he could not help asking.

"Hmm?" Saphy replied, deep in thought, before noticing him reading her back, "Oh, that. It's just a song lyric," she slid the towel further down to reveal the rest of the quote, "Oh mother, dear, we're not the fortunate ones", and, in doing so, revealed a little of her chest on the other side, "It's from Girls Just Wanna Have Fun."

"Cyndi Lauper?" he asked with surprise.

"Yes. What's wrong with Cyndi Lauper?" she became defensive, pulling the towel back up to cover both lines, grasping it against her chest just like the Venus statue at the Louvre.

"Nothing," Gabe said, worried she might close up to him, even while her inked body was most exposed, "It's just a bit surprising to see on you, that's all. This morning you were wearing a Rancid t-shirt. It's hard to square that with a love of 80s pop."

"Well, I'm a complicated woman, ok," she said, and Gabe could not help agreeing, "It's a great song and I agree with the sentiments. I can take inspiration in how I live my life from a pop song as much as from classical verse. It's true. All I really want is fun, but it's never that easy."

Gabe was impressed. She was, albeit warily, revealing a bit of herself to him, and he did not mean the flesh she was baring. He could tell that this could be the way to best understand her, to learn the meaning behind those things that she had decided to have permanently etched into herself. On one arm there was the now familiar female symbol, Venus' mirror, and, above it, a series of colourful rainbow stripes. The other arm was covered in Chinese figures. At the top, four symbols were in a row, a rectangular shape with a series of horizontal lines across it, another with a cross in the middle and then two far more complicated patterns.

"So, what does this one mean?" he asked, pointing to this row of Chinese letters, his finger nearly brushing against her wet skin.

"These are the Chinese symbols for free will," she replied, "It's to remind me always to take my own path and not be forced and guided by anybody else," she pointed to the next row, three more Chinese letters inked into her bicep, "And these are for stubbornness!" she laughed a little, "Yes, I know that's how I come across, but I have to stick to my own mind and not be led."

"Having spent a couple of days with you, I can't ever imagine you doing anything that wasn't your own choice," Gabe said, quite honestly.

"Yes, well, love makes fools of us all," she quoted in a kind of dismissive, offhand way that made Gabe suspect that she wanted to distract from her real feelings on the subject.

"How do you mean?" he pressed further.

"Since you've spent all this time in awe of the lovely Venus, you must know all she can do," she said, with a hint of sarcasm, "'Her mere gaze made Helen, who surpassed all mortals in beauty, readily bend and led her far from her path. It made her desert the best of men, forget her daughter and her dear parents.'"

"What's that from?" "It's the poet Sappho," she replied, "Forever my guiding light and greatest influence. See here."

She adjusted her position a little and opened her towel just a bit to show her thigh and the curve of her hip. Just above her waist, a series of Greek letters were inked in elegant calligraphy into her white skin. She ran her fingers over the markings with a sense of tenderness and regret.

"It says: 'I would rather see her warm supple step and the sparkle in her face than watch all the chariots in Lydia and foot soldiers armored in glittering bronze,'" she explained, "Those are the words Sappho used to describe her love, the most beautiful love there has ever been. It is a reminder to us all of how it should be."

"Is that why you have those tattoos?" Gabe asked, "To remind you?"

"I saw a film once where the hero was investigating a murder and had all the clues tattooed onto his body so he wouldn't forget them," she answered rather tangentially, "I always felt that was the way to be, indelibly branding yourself with what you are, where you've been and what you've done. Each of these marks is a memory, a reminder for me never to forget what I've learnt from life."

"So, what has love done to lead you astray?" Gabe asked, excited at how Saphy was suddenly being so open with him, in every possible way.

"See my broken heart," she said, turning toward him.

She lowered her towel a little so that some of her breast was on show, covering just the nipples. Above the left breast, there was a deep red heart tattooed onto her chest. A name had been inked into the middle that looked like it could have been "Anne", "Anna" or "Andy", but it had been obliterated, gouged out leaving a nasty looking scar.

"My first love," Saphy said, regretfully, running her finger along the scar, "I learned all about the madness of Venus the hard way. I did this to myself. As you may guess, it didn't work out so well!" "I'm sorry," he replied, genuinely, "What happened."

"We grew up," Saphy went on, "And grew apart. Society's conventions pushed her into a little box I didn't want to be inside."

"Well, I guess you had to stay true to your other tattoos!" he laughed, making her smile a little as well.

"And I'll always remain scarred and broken because of her," she said, "I'll always remember what she did to me."

"I thought you did that to yourself," Gabe pointed to her scarred heart.

"That's not the only scar she gave me," she said, "I've never shown this one to anyone before, but I feel like I can now."

Saphy opened her legs a little and showed him another tattoo that he would never have guessed was there on the inner thigh of her right leg. Gabe leant in to look closer at it, realising the strange awkwardness of being this close to the exposed flesh of a nearly naked young woman like this. Getting closer, Gabe could see that the line along her thigh was another nasty looking scar, but there were words tattooed into and against it, crudely scratched and inked into the skin, words like "dyke", "lez", "bitch". Underneath it, Saphy had tattooed "Sticks and stones can break my bones, but never break my soul".

"Yeah, I was one of those kids who was beaten up a lot in school," she grinned coldly, "But I always gave back as good as I got."

"Wow," Gabe replied, "I don't really know what to say to any of that."

He reached over and touched her thigh, gently and tenderly ran his finger along her scarring, seeking some understanding of her pain and angst. He felt her body tremble a little as his skin touched hers. Even though it was only the slightest touch of his finger, Gabe felt strangely intimate, running his digit over her thigh.

There was a sensation of life and excitement flowing through him that felt quite unusual out of his dreams.

After a moment, however, Saphy recovered her composure and seemed to feel she had revealed enough of herself. Gently pushing Gabe away, she wrapped the towel back tightly around her, covering the tattoos that were the most personal, the scars that ran deepest.

"Well, that's easily enough about me," she said, "I haven't told anyone nearly that much in years. I guess you're a good listener, but you've got to give something back. You've seen my broken heart, now what about yours?"

"None," he answered, slightly embarrassed, "I've never had my heart broken, never been in love. I have no scars about my body. I'm a blank page in an open book, an uncarved stone, unmoulded clay. I've never really done anything. This, these murders and mysteries, are the first exciting thing that has ever happened to me!"

"You know, that is probably more tragic than any number of broken hearts," Saphy replied, "You mean you've never even been with a woman?" "No," he admitted, "Never."

She looked at him with an expression of mixed surprise, pity and, perhaps, even a little tenderness. Maybe this new redheaded Saphy was a really different creature to the purple haired one. She certainly seemed more receptive and willing to share. Perhaps it was just that her life was truly in danger now. Seeming to have the same thought, Saphy shook off her sympathetic look and went back to her usual one.

"Well," she said, slightly joking but with a hard edge back in her voice, "When we're sharing that bed tonight, don't get any ideas. Remember that I like girls, ok?"

The sun beating down on his back, the sound of cool water tumbling and falling, the soft green grass beneath his bare feet, by now Gabe could recognise his recurring dream world. He knew that he was dreaming and he did not want to wake from it. In the dream world he felt good, he felt right. His body was no longer a mass of awkward aches and pains, but a soft, supple comfortable thing.

Instinctively, he felt himself drawn to the sound of water. He had been in this place before, he knew the attraction the water had to him. As he walked barefoot in the grass, he felt the presence of another body just behind him, although he seemed unable to turn to see it. Somehow he could tell that the other presence was none other than the goddess Venus. He could feel the force of her power flowing all over his naked body, making his skin tingle and all the hairs on his body stand on end.

Seeing the silver ripple of falling water in the fountain, Gabe walked toward it in a trance like state, still feeling the presence of the goddess over his shoulder. He stood beside the stone wall around the fountain's pool and looked into the clear water, watching the waves and ripples as the fountain's rain fell down into it. The presence behind him drew closer. He felt a soft hand on his naked back, the very touch of which caused him to become light headed and swoon.

"Come, my son, and look into my mirror," came the melodic voice ringing in Gabe's ears, "Come and see what the mirror has to tell you."

Gabe peered into the fountain, watched the ripples of the falling water, stared into it, becoming lost and detached from all around him until all he could see was waves on the water, and all he could here was falling splashes. As he drifted in this strange state, the waves began to form themselves into words and pictures, symbols and phrases.

At first, Gabe could make no sense of the swirling shapes. Patterns of lines and crosses formed and disappeared before his eyes before he could hope to decipher them. There was, however, a certain familiarity in these rows of shapes and symbols, he had seen them somewhere before. Gradually, those symbols started turning to letters, some recognisable ones and others from all kinds of different alphabets, and Gabe began to see individual words that he recognised.

One group of words stood out to him. It said "the fortunate ones", grew large in his vision and then burst into tiny lines, disappearing and reforming into other new letters. The phrase seemed familiar to him, but he could not remember from where and he had no time to think about it as he was faced with a new set of words and letters to try and understand.

The letters were all Greek, but they gradually transformed before Gabe's eyes into their English equivalent to reveal a phrase that read, quite cryptically, "I would rather see the sparkle in your face than watch the world in glittering copper or see foot soldiers armoured in hard iron." As Gabe stared, lost in the moment, baffled by the words he was seeing before him, the words grew to fill his field of vision until he could see nothing else.

As the words grew up before him, it became clear that the "o" of "copper" was, in actual fact, a circle with a cross beneath it, the symbol of Venus, her mirror. Soon, all that Gabe could focus on was just that individual word, the substance of the whole sentence seemed lost from his mind. The round surface of the mirror symbol shimmered as if it really were a metallic mirror itself. Eventually, that was the one and only thing that Gabe could see, filling the pool of the fountain, turning it into a flat, golden sheen with a completely reflective surface.

Gabe could now see his reflection in the polished metallic surface as he leaned over it. The shape of his body was becoming more and more defined in the mirror as all of the words, letters and symbols began to swirl around it. As he watched his reflection in the mirror began to change. It seemed to attract all the swirling shapes and symbols until they stuck against the mirror him, plastering the image with words and pictures like tattoos. One, in particular, caught his eye, a red heart that fluttered around like wings before attaching itself against the reflection of his chest.

Then, at that moment, he realised what he had been seeing. These abstract images and phrases were all drawn from the tattoos that he had seen on Saphy's body. Just as he thought that, the reflection began to change. His hair in the mirror pool became bright red, his body began to change shape, began to grow in the chest area until it showed breasts. He glanced down at his own body, but it was unchanged in any way. However, the image in the mirror was looking more and more like Saphy and less and less like Gabe. Yet it was still his reflection, when he moved his hand or turned his head, so did the image in the reflective surface.

"Remember," the melodic voice that made a tremble of excitement run down his spine uttered right into his head, "Remember that I like girls."

For a moment, Gabe felt the presence of the goddess stronger than ever, felt her hands running across his chest and thighs, leaving his body feeling more active and alive than it had been in a long while. He watched in the reflection as the image of Saphy, topless with a pair of pert, firm breasts, reached up and cupped her chest in her hands. Gabe realised that the reflection was, in fact, following his own hands, only he did not have a pair of breasts for himself.

His chest may have been completely flat to look down at, but his hands felt almost as if they were touching something real and fleshy. As he ran his hands over the imaginary mounds, he felt the sensation of nerves that were not really there running right up his spine. He watched as his reflection in Saphy's body began to fondle her breasts and began to feel the sensation of firm nipples between his fingers, getting perky and excited.

The same intense feeling of new sensations, of a body transformed, ran right down into his groin where he could feel his penis become erect again. There was something rubbing up against him that was making him become harder and harder, more and more aroused as he ran his fingers around his invisible chest and watched as Saphy in the mirror did the same. She opened her lips in an expression of pleasure that Gabe realised was his own and her eyes rolled back in her head.

He closed his eyes for a moment, savouring the intensity of the sensations he was feeling, and woke up. He was not in a field, naked beside a fountain, he was lying in bed in a cheap Parisian hotel beside an aggressive lesbian feminist. Despite the space in the double bed, he had moved around so much in his sleep that his body was pressed against hers, his groin against her thigh, rubbing up against her, giving him the arousal that was now highly embarrassing to him.

Beside him, Saphy began to stir and awaken, becoming aware, like Gabe a few minutes earlier, of her surroundings, becoming aware of the distressing arousal that her sleeping companion was displaying right up against her. She felt Gabe's body against hers and shivered away from him, sitting up and throwing back the blanket that covered both of them to look down at him shame-facedly trying to conceal the bulge in his pants.

"What the hell?" Saphy said, bleary eyed and just as irritable on waking as she was through a lot of the day, "Shit, I ask for one thing from you if we're sharing a bed. No funny stuff. And then I wake up to find you rubbing yourself against my leg with a massive boner, like some dog with no control over his actions whatsoever!"

"I...I...it's not my fault, I was asleep," Gabe stammered, blushing fiercely.

Saphy glared at him with an angry glint in her bright eyes, her flame red hair was even more messy and spiky from being slept on and gave her quite a sinister, threatening look that actually had Gabe retreating across to the other side of the bed. After a moment, however, her expression changed, her frown was transformed as her mouth creased into a smile and she let out a laugh of mixed mirth and triumph.

"Ha, you should see your face," she smirked, "I never knew I could be that terrifying. After all the murderers and secret societies of the last week, you're scared of being in bed with me?"

"Well, I'm not feeling immediately threatened by any of those other scary people."

"It's ok," she said, surprisingly reasonably, "I know that guys have no control over their bodies. I've known enough to know that you wake up like this all the time. It's nothing to do with me, right? I mean, it's not like you were having a sex dream about me or anything."

"Yeah, right," Gabe mumbled, blushing even deeper.

"Anyway, I think it's about time to get up," she went on, "We've got work to do. We're going back to the Louvre."

Gabe, however, could only think about his dream and what it meant. Did it tell him anything about the mystery or was it just his own hopes and fears? Had he really had a sex dream about Saphy? It did not seem that he felt that way about her. Sure, she was strangely fascinating, especially as she had opened up to him the day before, but he could not imagine lusting after her. No, he told himself, the dream did not mean he desired Saphy, just that he envied how confident and comfortable in her own body. That was why he had seen her in the mirror, wasn't it? Still, he had obviously been pretty aroused by the whole experience and Saphy had definitely been a part of it. Maybe it was just a sex dream.

Returning to the Louvre, the surroundings now felt familiar enough to Gabe that he no longer needed to follow Saphy's lead to find his way to the gallery where the Hermaphroditus statue lounged on his soft mattress. This familiarity would have been comforting to Gabe were he not such a complete bundle of nerves as to barely register that his feet were instinctively taking him in the right direction. He could not help replaying Atalanta's threat through his mind and imagining the eyes of all the white marble statues following him through the museum as he headed straight back to the one place to which he had been warned not to return.

Every statue of a towering goddess armed and poised to strike, he imagined was one of the murderous naiads about to deal out to him the same treatment that they had to the poor victim at the National Gallery back in London. He could barely concentrate on what Saphy was saying about the mystery as his attention continually darted around the room in search of anything out of the ordinary.

Both the previous times he had encountered Atalanta and the naiads, they had appeared and disappeared silently, with barely a flutter of white fabric for him to notice. This scared him more than anything, the idea that they could suddenly be there just where he was looking without him ever seeing them arrive. For all he knew, they could be there watching him right now. His back twitched and tingled, half expecting to be impaled with the shaft of a deadly arrow at any moment.

Saphy, however, seemed exhilarated by the whole situation. While Gabe glanced around silently and nervously, Saphy was more talkative than he had ever seen her. The mystery and danger seemed to suit her and find her in her element. Gabe did not know whether this newfound chattiness and enthusiasm was just a different reaction to nervous fear to his, or whether she was genuinely excited. Whatever the reason, as they approached the reclining nude hermaphrodite once more, Saphy was in full flow with her latest idea.

"I've been reading some of the books that I, er, borrowed from the library back in Cambridge," she was explaining as they crossed the red and white squares of the gallery floor, "I think we've been looking in the wrong place. It's not the statue itself that holds the clue."

"What? How do you mean?" Gabe asked, distractedly half listening as he suspiciously eyed up the statue of Diana with her quiver full of arrows, "If it's not the statue why are we here? Why are we putting ourselves in danger?"

"It's not the statue. It's the mattress he's lying on."

"Huh?"

"The statue dates right back to the Roman period, but the mattress doesn't," she explained, "It was made after the statue's rediscovery in the 1600s, the time that all of Europe suddenly became excited about the Hermaphroditus and Salmacis legend. If any part of the statue is going to leave us a clue, it's that."

"Why that part, specifically?"

"Because of the artist that made it. Cardinal Borghese commissioned his protege, a young sculptor named Gian Lorenzo Bernini to create the mattress. Bernini went on to become the leading sculptor and architect in all of Italy. And, here's the interesting part..."

"What?" "Bernini was rumoured to be a member of the Illuminati, the secret society, and could not resist containing all manner of coded clues and suggestions in his sculptures. The mattress here is one of his earliest works. If he had any knowledge of the secret of Salmacis, he is bound to have left his mark, left us a clue somewhere."

"OK, but where?" Gabe was beginning to get hooked in by Saphy's excitement, beginning to get interested in the mystery at the expense of his caution, "We can't just turn over all the buttons on the mattress without attracting some suspicion."

"Hmmm, good point," she agreed, "Still, that's a good idea about the buttons. That's probably the best place to hide something. If we could just prize one up without the guard noticing."

"We could distract him somehow, but that would still only give us time to see one." "Which one?" she bent over to get a closer look along the mattress, "Are there any that look different, that look loose somehow."

"Wait a minute," Gabe said, staring at the statue and replaying the number of times they had seen that pose over the last few days, "Just think, where did we first see this? What led us here in the first place? The painting. The Rokeby Venus."

"I see, that painting was painted at the same time as this mattress was made. You think that the painting gives a suggestion about where we can find our next clue here."

"Exactly. Didn't Professor Cavendish say something about the painting not being finished? Something that seemed like a deliberate case of leaving it, drawing attention to one particular spot."

"Yes," Saphy said, excitedly, "That's right. The area around the left foot."

Both of their eyes shot instantly down the bare left leg of the naked marble statue to where its left foot rested daintily on the soft looking mattress. Sure enough, one of the mattress buttons lay right there. Both began to look pretty excited about what they might discover beneath it. There was just one problem.

"So, how do we distract the guard long enough to look beneath it?" Gabe broke the excited moment to ask.

"I'll take care of that," Saphy replied with a little smirk on her face, "You just be ready to overturn that button and snap a photo with that ever present camera."

Saphy walked across the other side of the room and Gabe followed her with his eyes, wondering just what she was going to do. The gallery was quiet but not completely empty. A handful of other people were browsing around the various statues and the guard was pacing up and down. Saphy positioned herself on the opposite side of the gallery looking back over at Gabe. She smiled and winked at him in a way that was oddly suggestive given their relationship up to this point.

Gabe looked around the room once more. Suddenly all the eyes were turned away from him, the guard turned and hurried across the room to where Saphy was standing. Gabe knew that he may only have a few seconds and therefore resisted the urge to follow where everybody's attention was turned. Instead, he ducked under the barrier and quickly grabbed the button of the mattress.

Despite his expectations, Gabe was still a little surprised that the button was just loosely fitted inside and came up easily in his hand. There was certainly something scratched into the underside of the button, maybe letters or words, but over time they had worn down as to be almost invisible. Still, knowing he only had a moment, Gabe took his camera and snapped a quick picture before replacing the button and ducking back beneath the barrier.

As he breathed a sigh of relief to have managed all this quickly and smoothly without being caught, Gabe allowed himself a moment to glance up and see just what had caused such a distraction that let him do it. He could not help gasping with surprise as he looked across the room to see the guard sternly having words with Saphy, who had her shirt lifted to expose a pair of round, bare breasts. Gabe got a brief glimpse of the disfigured heart tattoo and the shining glimmer of a nipple piercing, before her chest was covered once more. As the guard showed her out of the gallery, Saphy turned to Gabe and gave him a cheeky smile and a thumb up sign. Gabe, blushing and unsure just what to do, could only mirror her and give the same sign back.

They met up again beneath the glass pyramid where Gabe found Saphy sat waiting for him with a look of triumph on her face. Gabe sat down beside her with his camera out and for a moment was completely speechless.

"Works every time," Saphy said, breaking the silence, "If women's bodies are going to be so objectified then we women should make use of that. It can give us the power sometimes."

"I have to say, that was not what I was expecting when you promised to provide a distraction," Gabe replied, honestly.

"Yeah, well it was the simplest, quickest thing I could think of," she admitted, "So, what did you find?"

He passed her the camera with the image of the scratchings on the underside of the button brought up on the viewing screen.

"Well, it's definitely something," she said, with a tone of disappointment, "But I guess we can't really quite see what."

"Just a minute," he replied, taking the camera back.

He had had an idea. Adjusting the contrast of light and shadow with the controls on his camera would make the scratchings much better defined within the photograph. Sure enough, after a few adjustments, a group of Greek letters began to emerge, still worn and faded but clearly spelling out a word, the letters in the middle pretty obvious while the ones on either end harder to read.

"Artemis!" Saphy exclaimed when she saw it, "That's what it looks like."

"What's Artemis?" Gabe asked.

"Artemis is the Greek word for Diana," she explained, "The virgin goddess worshipped by the naiads. That doesn't really tell us anything. Why would they reveal themselves and their involvement to stop us from discovering this? It doesn't make any sense."

"Maybe that isn't what it means," Gabe suggested.

"But, what else could it be except Artemis?" Saphy asked.

"Beats me, you're the expert here," he replied, "Are you sure there aren't some other Artemises?"

"Artemises? No," she replied, before appearing to have a brainwave, "Although...Where did your Professor Gerard say that the Fountain of Salmacis was supposed to be?" "Oh, um, I can't remember the name of it," he said, "One of the wonders of the world. It was in Turkey."

"The Mausoleum?"

"Yeah, that sounds like it. Why?"

"Because the woman who had it built was called Artemisia."

"What does that mean?"

"It means that we're going to Turkey!" Saphy announced as they both sprung to their feet together and left the museum.

Back beneath the pyramid, there was a movement in the shadows. Gabe might have become distracted from his fear of being watched, but that did not mean the fear was any less appropriate. The figures lurking in shadows had been following him right from the moment that he was nervously scanning the room for them. Now that

Gabe and Saphy had left, the figures in the shadows moved and also hurried towards the exit.

CHAPTER 2

There were two of them, both dressed archaically in flowing robes, one a woman in white, the other a man in black. The woman had long waves of dark hair, wore a tunic and carried a quiver of arrows, one of which had been drawn on her bow and directed straight at her opposite number. Opposite, in a long black robe marked with a white cross, with a gun drawn against the naiads bow, Gabe might have been surprised to see Detective Inspector Gilbert of the Cambridge CID. Gilbert left the Louvre and, rather than following Gabe and Saphy, hailed a cab and headed off in the opposite direction.

The Grand Prior of Villeneuve arrived in a bad mood. He had just flown back into France that morning and that never made him very happy. He hated having to share the confined, enclosed space of an aircraft with all those sweating, screaming, chattering people even for such a small space of time as this. In general, the Prior felt that one of the advantages of being in a position of such importance as his was that in when in command you could send other people to do the travelling and the work for you while you directed them from home and comfort. He had always seen himself as more of a planner than a doer. He was the brains, the visionary, other people were there to enact his plans. Still, the situation now was such that he felt he needed perhaps to take on a more hands on approach.

At least his office here was appropriately grand and offered him the requisite level of comfort after his unpleasant journey. It was a large, expansive space where he sat at a grand chair that was almost more like a throne. The walls were lined with the Prior's private library of mediaeval and early modern texts, many of them the only copies containing the Order's history and secrets. His large oak desk had, perched on top of it, a giant gold bird of prey encrusted with jewels. The Prior sat himself down in the chair and began to think things through.

He had to admit that he had underestimated that shy, effeminate photographer and his angry girl companion. Of all the people that had coming searching for the secret of Salmacis over the years, these seemed far the least likely to succeed. And yet they had managed to make their way this far. The Prior was beginning to suspect that these two unlikely mystery solvers might just have that different outlook that it would take to discover the Fountain once and for all. He was starting to think that maybe it would be better to keep them alive just that little bit longer, just out of curiosity to see what they did next.

He did not usually have any regrets about the tough decisions that he had had to make. He knew that everything that he did was for the greater good, to restore the Order to their former position of glory and power and maybe something greater. He knew that the world would be a better place with the Order being in control, there would be moral discipline and things would be done in the right way in the right place. The power would be theirs, would be his, to set things right, to bring back the traditional values and ways of living.

It was unfortunate what happened to Professor White, but it was a necessary evil. Deaths did not bother the Prior like they did some smaller minded people, because he could see where they fit into the grander plan and where they would serve a greater purpose. Eventually, he knew, he would look back on the whole incident as having been part of that which allowed the Order finally to fulfil its destiny.

He never usually had regrets, however he was starting to feel he may have been a little hasty in hiring those brutal twin assassins, the men calling themselves Phobus and Deimus. He was a man that liked to be in control and he was learning that these two were harder to control than he had hoped. The very reason he had hired them, their brutality, their ruthless determination to see things through, their utter lack of any compassion or more gentle traits and their single minded moral code, made them almost impossible to contradict.

He had heard stories about these two that he barely believed, but now was not so sure about, it was said that they had ritually castrated themselves out of disdain for feelings of sexual desire. They were supposed to loathe sexuality in all its forms more than anything else. That partly scared the Prior. Of course, he knew that homosexuality was an abomination, that men and women had a place that they needed to keep to, but he also knew that sexual relations between men and women were both necessary and an important part of reinforcing power relations. The single mindedness displayed by the twins took none of that into account. They saw everything in black and white, where the Prior appreciated that everything was really about appropriately manipulating shades of grey.

Unlike him, they saw death, violence and chaos as important for their own sake, they did not understand the bigger picture or the greater good. The Prior had always been convinced of the worth of what he was doing and was a little put off at having to work with men even he thought to be doing wrong. Just look at how difficult it had been for him to get them to not kill the boy in Cambridge. They had been so determined to do it and would not understand how having him alive to take blame for the murders would suit the bigger picture far better.

There was a knock on the door and in came one of his many robed acolytes. Drawing back his hood, the newcomer revealed himself as Detective Inspector Gilbert. The Prior had relied on Gilbert in Cambridge to engineer the evidence to suggest the boy as the murderer of Professor Cavendish and, as a result, had had to include the detective in his plans rather more than he would otherwise have done. After his rage at discovering the two amateur mystery solvers had left the country, he had sent Gilbert to find them.

"You had better be bringing me good news, Gilbert," the Prior said, with a sneer in his French accented English.

"I've found them," came the reply, "They went to the Louvre, as predicted, they're searching for clues on the statue."

"Good," the Prior smiled, they were following the same predictable course as everyone else who had searched for the secret in the past, there was not much to discover there, "And now?"

"They found something, a clue," said Gilbert with a certain amount of surprise.

"Really?" the Prior's sneering tone continued, "Interesting...Maybe they're more capable than we gave them credit for. And what did they learn?"

"Nothing we don't know already, they're headed for the Mausoleum. It will be easy to ensure that they have a little accident along the way. I've looked into it and there's nobody back in England that would much miss either of them."

"No, Gilbert, we'll wait," the Prior came to a decision that, for once, he was not completely sure of, "We'll wait and watch. They discovered a secret in the statue, perhaps we can use their skills, their different style of deduction, to make new discoveries of our own. Keep them alive unless they get too close."

His earlier thoughts seemed confirmed by Gilbert's observations. He had misjudged, somewhat unusual for him, and now he was ready to admit his mistake and work from it. He had underestimated these two and he was not about to do that again. If they wanted to solve the mystery then the Prior was quite happy to let them, provided he could ensure that if they should discover the secret it should come rather into his power than theirs.

"One more thing," Gilbert came in with, just as the Prior was about to dismiss him, "We're not the only ones watching. The naiads are onto them too."

"Good, good," the Prior smiled strangely, "Keep track of them too. If we can get ourselves one of them then we may not need any other help anyway."

"So, what now?" Gilbert asked.

"Now, I think we need to get ourselves to Turkey. Another tiresome bit of air travel, it would seem, and just when I had got settled here. Assemble a team and try to find the next flight out of here."

"Would those two eunuch assassins be a part of that team?" Gilbert said with a shudder of both disgust and fear.

"Hmm, yes, I think we made need their unique abilities if we are to capture a naiad," the Prior considered, "You'd better inform them as well, but we'll have to keep them in check until we need them."

As Gilbert left, the Prior allowed himself a smile despite the loathsome prospect of another plane journey. All the pieces were beginning to come together. These two kids might just be the catalyst for a discovery that the Order had waited centuries for, for their return to power and glory.

On a peninsula of dry land surrounded by deep blue seas and bright blue skies, the town of Bodrum has become in recent years a magnet for tourists seeking the sunshine and beautiful beaches of the Aegean Sea. The thousands of people who come from across the world to enjoy the universal sunshine of this stretch of coast are mostly unconcerned by the region's history. However, the peninsula's location on the southern part of Turkey's coast has made it strategically important for thousands of years. Before the tourist boom in the 20th century, the town was mostly populated by fishermen and sponge divers. However, a series of stern, square greystone towers overlooking the harbour give a suggestion of the peninsula's role as a stronghold in the age of the crusaders.

This castle was built on a site that had always been at the heart of the defences of the region. When in ancient times this was the kingdom of Caria, the ruling kings had their base here as well. It was here, in Halicarnassus, beside the modern town of Bodrum that the greatest of those rulers was buried in a grand Mausoleum whose construction and beautiful statues made Antipater of Sidon name it as one of his legendary Seven Wonders of the World.

Antipater's list, however, was written for the travellers of the second century BC and the Mausoleum that confronted Gabe and Saphy looked considerably less impressive as they arrived in Bodrum after a number of uncomfortable train journeys across France, Germany, Austria, Hungary, Romania, Bulgaria and finally into Turkey after two days of travel. Given their need to be careful with money and the fact that using trains and other methods they could cross European borders without showing their passports, handy when they were still wanted by the authorities in England, they had had to rule out the much simpler option of a flight direct from Paris, resulting in their slow, uncomfortable journey and other nights sharing a bed in tiny cheap hotels in Budapest and Istanbul.

Despite all of this, Saphy had proved, for the most part despite occasional grumpy spells, to be far better company than Gabe had experienced on the journey from London. Solving the latest mystery seemed to have distracted her enough from her anger at the death of Jane Cavendish, her mentor, that she seemed in much better spirits.

That they had worked well together in the Louvre to uncover the latest clue meant that she was also beginning to trust Gabe more and to share her thoughts with him. There had not, however, been a moment of such intimacy as they had shared in the Paris hotel room. Saphy, although more open with Gabe now, was keen to talk classical history and not her own history or feelings. During the journey, she had been happy to read the many books she had taken from Cambridge and had passed the time explaining to Gabe about the Mausoleum of Halicarnassus and its history.

"It was a tomb built for Mausolus, the ruler of Caria," she had explained as the train rumbled through Turkish hills, "We use the word mausoleum for all types of tombs these days, but that's where the word comes from, it was named after Mausolus. He was a satrap, a regional ruler in the Persian Empire. However, he was a greater admirer of Greek culture and the Greek way of life. He built a number of new Greek style cities along the coast. He also decided to move his capital from Mylasa, the old Persian capital of his ancestors, to Halicarnassus, where he could build a grand city of gleaming marble in the Greek style to reflect Mausolus' greatness as a king.

"Artemisia was Mausolus' sister, but, according to the rules of the Carian royal family, she also became his wife."

"Euhhh," Gabe made a disgusted noise, "That's pretty weird."

"It was fairly normal among royal families back then, they didn't want to dilute the royal bloodline," Saphy explained, "Hey, even today's royal families tend to marry their cousins and end up a bit inbred. Why do you think they're all so thick and funny looking?"

"Any of that sort of thing in your own aristocratic family?" Gabe couldn't help asking, but, when his companion had given him a frosty look, he had turned the conversation back to the ancients, "So, they were brother and sister forced to become husband and wife? I bet that was a bit of an awkward marriage."

"Not at all, apparently she was utterly devoted to him and the successes of their reign were partly down to how they ruled together. They were almost like two halves of same whole. Artemisia's grief on the death of her husband is legendary. Over the two years after he died, she continued to rule the country, winning a famous victory over the people of Rhodes through her shrewd tactical command, but she pined constantly for her dead husband and wasted away and died herself within those two years. According to legend, she mixed her husband's ashes in with her daily drink every morning so that they could truly become one together." "Wow, that's pretty hardcore weird," Gabe responded, "It kind of tips over from being romantic into being creepy."

"But, that's not all she did for the memory of her beloved husband. She also decided to build him a tomb that would be the most incredible monument to his greatness and to their love. She sent for all the greatest artists, designers and sculptors from across Greece and they came and built this great marble tomb.

"'A huge flight of stone steps led up to it, flanked by stone lions and statues of gods and goddesses,'" she read from one of her books, "'The tomb itself was over 130 feet high and guarded by stone warriors on horseback at each of the corners. The bas-reliefs depicted battles with centaurs and amazon warrior women. The huge, heavy pyramidal roof was topped with a quadriga, a chariot pulled by four huge horses in which stood the figures of Mausolus and Artemisia together.' "Look, there's a picture," she turned in the narrow, hard seat of the railway carriage to show Gabe the image, a modern recreation of the grand tomb.

"That's really something," Gabe marvelled, "But I remember Professor Gerard saying that it was destroyed."

"That's right," she confirmed, "Artemisia was succeeded by her sister Ada, but the city was besieged and conquered by Alexander the Great. The Mausoleum, however, survived this and attacks by pirates as the city declined in importance. However, a series of earthquakes six hundred years ago brought the whole weight of the roof and the bronze chariot crashing down.

"Still, the design has been copied and recreated hundreds of times in other buildings, in other times. Look at this," she showed him another, very similar looking picture, "That's the Masonic House of the Temple in Washington. The design is styled on the Mausoleum. It would seem that our white cross wearers aren't the first secret society interested in it!" "So, it's in ruins then?" said Gabe, fascinated that he had heard so much about the Seven Wonders of the World down the years without really having any idea about what those wonders had been.

"Yeah, the earthquake pretty much destroyed it," Saphy confirmed, "Most of the Seven Wonders failed to last into modern times. The only one that's still in tact is the pyramids."

Even this warning of the Mausoleum no longer bearing much resemblance to its glory days could not prepare Gabe for the disappointment of seeing the ruins on their eventual arrival in Bodrum. A pile of rocks would, perhaps, be a generous description for the remaining ruins of the Mausoleum. A random spread of rocks, not even showing vague foundations, would be more accurate. There was almost literally nothing to be seen at the site of this once great tomb. Even Saphy, who had read up on it extensively before arriving, looked disappointed that there was not more there.

The bright light of the sun was almost blinding after the drizzling grey of London and Paris and two days inside a train carriage. Gabe rubbed his eyes and stared at the rocks in front of him as if doing so could conjure up an image of the Mausoleum's former greatness. He could not quite believe they had travelled all this way to see this. He did not quite know what they planned to do now they were here. His travelling companion appeared almost as unsure herself.

Saphy, her flame red hair matching the flushed look her pale English skin had taken on in the Turkish heat, fanned herself with one of her books. She was dressed in the ever present big black biker boots, a short denim mini-skirt and a baggy white t-shirt with "The Slits" written across the front. It was torn in a number of places and held together with safety pins that shone brightly in the hot sun. She began to wander among the slight ruins, idly eyeing up each of the stones as if they might yield their secrets that way.

"This is it?" Gabe said, breaking the disappointed silence.

"Yeah, this is all that's left," the letdown in her voice palpably echoed his, "No wonder nobody thinks there's anything left to find."

"What are we even looking for?" he asked, a note of frustration adding to his disappointment.

"Well, I don't know, do I?" Saphy's voice betrayed that aggressive streak that had seemed a little subdued over the last two or three days, "Do you expect me to always have all the answers?"

"Well, it was your idea to come here!"

"What else was I supposed to get from that fucking useless clue you uncovered?" she demanded, "It's just one word."

"I guess it was stupid of me to trust to your brilliant mind," he threw back angrily, the midday sun beating down on his sweating forehead was making him uncomfortable and irritable, "Stupid of me to think that we might actually be getting somewhere!"

He wiped the sweat from his brow and stormed off across to the other side of the ruins. Crouching down in the relative shade behind one of the larger rocks, he pretended to study it for any new signs or clues. In reality, he was upset and angry, with himself, with the heat, with the mystery they were failing to solve, basically with everything. More than anything, however, he felt annoyed at Saphy, more than he thought he ever would. He had not imagined the aggressive moods that he had seen in her from the first could upset him this much. Then, something happened that he had expected even less.

"I'm sorry," said Saphy from behind him, much to Gabe's surprise, not just at the fact that she had come up silently upon him as he was deep in thought about her, but also the fact that she had actually apologised, something he had never seen as the result of any of her angry moods before, "I think we got a little carried away there. Must be the heat or something. Anyway, I think we've been doing really well to get this far and I certainly couldn't have done it on my own. So, I guess what I'm saying is that I'm sorry for all the aggressive way that I behave sometimes, because actually I think we make a bloody good team and I think that if we work together we might really have a chance of cracking this thing. So, how about it, want to see what more we can dig up?"

She reached out her hand to him and pulled him to his feet, brushing the dusty Turkish soil from his trousers. Oddly, apart from that moment of intimacy in the Paris hotel room, this was the most physical contact that they had had in all the short time that they had known each other. Once again, like that moment, Gabe felt a sense of stripping away the layers of Saphy's complex personality to see the fragile, caring person beneath it all.

"Thanks, Saphy," he said, "I guess we can work pretty well together sometimes. Come on, there's a little museum over there. We've been good at museums before, maybe that's more the place to start."

After the grand international museums that Gabe and Saphy's mysteries had taken them to in London and Paris, the Halicarnassus Mausoleum Museum seemed inordinately small. In reality it was just a few rooms with what little statuary could be salvaged from the rubble outside and had not been taken away to somewhere like London's British Museum, along with lots of information and reconstructive images of what the Mausoleum may once have looked like. In all, they were able to look around the whole museum in about half an hour.

"'When the crusading knights built the Castle, they took stone from the Mausoleum ruins to fortify it,'" Saphy read in one of the displays, happy to note that this Turkish museum was more willing to write explanations in English than the museums in England were to use any other languages, "'In 1522, further fortifications at the

Castle came as a result of a rumoured invasion from the Turkish sultan Suleiman the Magnificent. The Crusaders broke up what remained of the tomb and built it into their walls. The Mausoleum's polished marble can still be seen today in the Castle towers.'"

"So, I guess if there's anything for the stones to tell us, then maybe we shouldn't be looking in the ruins here," Gabe suggested.

"Right, there's actually more parts of the Mausoleum at the Castle than there is here," she confirmed, "So that's where we're headed."

They walked back down towards the sea through Bodrum town, heading for the obvious focal point of the historic settlement. For a building some of which was over five hundred years old, Bodrum Castle remains remarkably in tact and unchanged and, as the two amateur mystery solvers arrived at the curve of the high grey curtain wall and looked up at the imposing perfect battlements and crenellations, they could well imagine what stern defensive deterrent the fort offered for any mediaeval warrior foolish enough to lay siege to it.

They walked in through one of the many gates in this outer wall and were confronted by the interior of the castle, still almost as well preserved as it appeared from the outside. Red and white crosses were still visible in the glass of the windows, cannons still stood in their places along the ramparts, pointing out to sea. A number of square grey towers stood around the castle site, seemingly arranged in an almost random assembly, some much closer and at different angles to the others. Each tower was designed in a slightly different style. Around the walls, the carved designs, coats of arms and relief images, were still clearly outlined. Amongst all of this, the marble of the former Mausoleum was obvious, its images of centaurs and amazons now forming part of the Castle's decorations.

They approached one of the towers. It was about three storeys high and featured a simple set of carved designs part way up. Close to the top of the tower, they could see the long reclining figure of a white lion beneath another coat of arms. However, their attention was distracted by another carving, closer to the ground, something disturbingly familiar. It was a cross, with the four points narrow at the centre and growing wider at the ends like inverted triangle shapes. It was a symbol that Gabe had seen on the robes of the men that had captured and locked him up in Cambridge, the ones who had ties to the creepy hissing voiced bald assassins, the ones who had been responsible for the death of Professor Cavendish.

"Look," Saphy pointed, "Recognise that?" "All too well," Gabe agreed, "But what does it mean?"

"It's a Maltese cross," came the interjection of another voice, a precise, pronounced accent speaking clipped if perfect English, "Symbol of the Sovereign Order of Saint John of Jerusalem, the Knights Hospitaller."

They turned in surprise to see the figure standing beside them, dressed in casual slacks and a polo neck shirt, the sun glinting off his high forehead with beads of sweat on his thinning grey hair. His eyes studied them with a close scrutiny, as if he was equally surprised to see them in front of him and was trying to figure out quite how they had got there. It was Dr. Raymond Gerard, the classics professor from Pembroke College, Cambridge.

"Dr. Gerard?" said Gabe with an expression of confusion on his face, "Aren't you supposed to be in England? What are you doing here?"

"Mr. Herrison, I might ask you the same question, but I assume you are here for the same reason as myself and through following the same line of reasoning," he said, his eyes looking piercingly into Gabe's, "After you came to my office with your wild ideas about Robert and the Fountain of Salmacis, I was inspired to look a little closer into my colleague's research. I think that he may have been close to finding something when his unfortunate disappearance occurred. I have followed the clues that he left here in the hope of finishing his work."

"You mean, you believe there is a fountain to discover?"

"Do not misunderstand me, Mr. Herrison, I do not mean to suggest that I believe in magic or the supernatural transformative abilities of legend. However, if Robert has some evidence of a real find of classical historic significance, I would like to discover it. His research suggests that he uncovered some clues in the 17th century Hermaphroditus statue that led him here. It was a version of that same statue that you were so interested in, the one you talked to Jane Cavendish about." "Well, isn't that just great?" Saphy interjected, a note of aggressive sarcasm in her voice, "We're all here now on the same little quest. How about we help each other out?"

"Miss Cross, I don't believe we've been properly acquainted with one another," Dr. Gerard gave her his hand to shake, with Saphy took after a few seconds' consideration, "I have heard great things about you from Jane. What tragic circumstances for the college to lose one of its great unconventional thinkers. I had a lot of respect for Jane even though her ideas were sometimes a little unusual."

"She was a brilliant mind, a true inspiration, something I'm sure you could have gained from her if you'd given her the chance," Saphy pouted aggressively, "Anyway, let's try not to dwell on it. In the absence of your infinitely more useful colleague, I guess we're going to ask for your help once more. What does the cross mean?"

"Like I said, it was the symbol of the Knights Hospitaller, the order of Crusader knights that first built the Castle here at Bodrum" he explained, "It was designed so each edge of the cross has two points, making eight in total, representing the eight tongues of the Order."

"Tongues?" asked Gabe, confused.

"Like provinces in other orders," Dr. Gerard went on, "The tongues of the Hospitallers were the subgroups of the Order, representing the various Grand Priories of the different geographical regions of the Hospitaller Order, Provence, Auvergne, France, Aragon, Castile, Italy, England and Germany. The eight towers of the castle here also represent the eight tongues. Each tongue was responsible for their own tower, and the defence and maintenance of the castle area around it, hence the differing architectural styles and symbols. The Lion Tower here is the tower of the English tongue. The tallest one over there is the French as the Order was always most powerful in France."

"And this Order, were they knights or priests?" Gabe asked, "I don't really understand." "The Hospitallers were a monastic order," Dr. Gerard explained, "They were responsible for the hospital in Jerusalem that was built for the Christian pilgrims in mediaeval times.

However, the pilgrimage proved a dangerous journey for the pilgrims so the monks of the Hospitaller Order soon provided an armed escort."

"So the monks became an army?"

"Exactly, an army of God, separate from any country or government. They won many great victories for the Christian world against the Muslim armies during the Crusades and this made them grow rich and powerful. They were not just independent from any government by then, they wielded more power than many governments."

"How much power?"

"You've heard of the Knights Templar, right?" Dr. Gerard asked and Gabe remembered hearing that name in connection with various conspiracies and legends, "They were the other major Order of monastic knights. The incredible power and wealth that they held has caused many to speculate that they had access to all kinds of ancient secrets. They were so powerful that in the 1300s the King of France and the Pope had their leaders arrested and executed and the Order shut down. Who were the main people to benefit from this? The Hospitallers. Most of their property and thus much of their wealth ended up in the hands of the Hospitallers, who were now the uncontested power of knightly orders, even though their original purpose had long since ended with the 12th century fall of Jerusalem.

"Despite that fact, they just grew more powerful and richer throughout the middle ages. They controlled much of the Mediterranean from their base in Rhodes and were able to expand outwards, building numerous castles like this one to safeguard their position of importance."

"So, what happened to them?"

"Like anybody who rises to a position of power and authority, like the Templars before them, the Hospitallers attracted greedy eyes determined to usurp their role. The powerful Turkish sultan Suleiman the Magnificent laid siege to them in Rhodes and defeated them. That was when they left this castle. This was the end of the Hospitallers position as the great power in the region, but their wealth was still enough that they were able to occupy the island of Malta where they settled afterwards. Now, they became less a religious crusading order and more a group of mercenaries, serving in foreign navies and defending sailors against piracy in exchange for great sums of money.

"Many feel that the Hospitallers lost their way in this time, failing to react to the growing power of Islam and the Catholic church's struggle with the increase in Protestantism, they were no longer an Order devoted to fighting for the holy against the immoral, they were now solely concerned with making money. When Napoleon took Malta, the Order ceased to exist in any real sense."

"So, the Order no longer exists?" Gabe asked, knowing that, whatever Dr. Gerard said, their power was perhaps not so completely in the past as he had heard, he knew from seeing that cross once more that in some way this Order of mediaeval warrior monks still asserted an influence on events today.

"In some sense it does, yes," Dr. Gerard replied, "The Sovereign Military Order of Malta in the modern day claim descent from the Knights Hospitaller and their original mission. They offer aid and assistance to the sick and diseased and victims of natural disasters. However, there are those who feel that the Order of Malta's offer of aid to all regardless of race or religion contradicts the Hospitaller origin as a Christian crusading Order. The lack of authenticity in the Order of Malta did bring on a few mimic Orders claiming to represent the true will of the Hospitallers in the 20th century. Who knows? Maybe some of these continue to operate."

"Well, that's all very interesting," Saphy, usually the one most keen on getting an impromptu history lesson, was now operating almost entirely with abrasive sarcasm, "But what has that possibly got to do with the Fountain of Salmacis, apart from the chance of the Hospitallers happening to build their Castle in roughly the same place as Salmacis might have been?" "Oh it's a much more significant choice of location than that," Dr. Gerard responded, "Robert theorised that the Fountain of Salmacis was the whole reason for the Hospitallers to have chosen this spot for their Castle; that this Castle was, in actual fact, built to defend that secret rather than for strategic purposes. The power of Salmacis could prove a valuable secret for any army in time of war. Just imagine it, the ability to transform the enemies' greatest, strongest warriors into weak and feeble women."

"Yeah, 'cause women can't possibly handle themselves in a fight," Saphy chipped in snarkily.

"Robert suggested that in 1522, when Suleiman the Magnificent was about to seize control of the Hospitaller lands, they destroyed the remaining ruins of the Mausoleum not to fortify the Castle further, but rather to destroy any evidence of Salmacis' existence."

"Surely if the Hospitallers used magical feminising transformations against their enemies, then history would record something that bizarre," Saphy added.

"As I already mentioned on more than one occasion, there is no such thing as such a magical transformation," Dr. Gerard finally seemed to become a little irritated by Saphy's snide interjections, "The Hospitallers may have believed in the power, but they were more concerned about guarding it lest it come into the wrong hands, than in using it themselves."

"So, if they destroyed all evidence of Salmacis' location five hundred years ago, what is it that you hope to find here?" Gabe asked.

"The Hospitallers were determined such secrets should not be lost completely," Dr. Gerard explained, "They made sure that by following the right path people could discover them. Robert felt that, in destroying the Mausoleum ruins, the Hospitallers hid their secret in the marble built into these towers here."

"Well, that's just what we were looking for anyway," Saphy replied, "But if you want to join in and lend a hand, then you're welcome to." "How come all those towers are bunched closer together and then there's a big space down to the wall there?" Gabe wondered, "It doesn't seem like the strongest defensive position."

"As I said before, each tower and the area around it was the responsibility of each different tongue of the Order," Dr. Gerard told him, "Perhaps the English and French tongues did not organise themselves well enough, perhaps some sort of internal rivalries."

"So, wait, that one with the lion is England, right?" Saphy asked, "And the tall one's France?"

"That is correct," Dr. Gerard confirmed.

"Right, so which is which of the others then?"

"That's Auvergne and Provence, the two there behind France, Castile and Aragon on the other side, and that's Germany and down there is Italy." "Auvergne and Provence, those are parts of France as well, right?" Saphy asked, "So, why is there a separate one for France?"

"France was so powerful within the Order that they had control of three tongues, France in the north, Auvergne centrally and Provence in the south."

"And Castile and Aragon, those are the two halves of Spain," Saphy added.

"Indeed. And where are you going with this, Miss Cross?" Dr. Gerard's tone was becoming a little superior.

"How come the three French towers are grouped close together, as are the two Spanish ones?"

"Perhaps the French tongues were more comfortable being close to each other rather than Germany or England," Gabe suggested.

"What about you, the brilliant Cambridge University academic, why do you think they're configured like that?" Saphy turned her sarcasm onto Dr. Gerard.

"I have absolutely no idea what you're suggesting."

"Think about it, France bunched up over there," she pointed to the towers, "England here and Spain there. They're arranged geographically, the castle is laid out like a map!"

"So?"

"So, if we know the whereabouts of England, France and Spain on this map, we can extrapolate the position of Turkey," Saphy explained, a note of triumph evident in her voice as if she was competitively trying to solve the mystery against Dr. Gerard, "And if we can find the spot that represents Bodrum, then that's the place to be looking for our clues."

"Great," said Gabe, excitably, "So, all we need to know is the distance from two places in reality and then factor it down to the distances here in the castle." "There is about 400 kilometres between Provence and Auvergne," Dr. Gerard interrupted, "And a further 2500 kilometres from Auvergne, through Italy to get to Turkey."

"How would you even know that just off the top of your head?" Saphy asked sulkily.

"I've had a whole education," the university professor replied smugly to the drop-out, unconsciously echoing a similar phrase with which she herself had once dismissed Gabe's own lack of knowledge.

"Right, ok, all we have to do then is pace out the distance between the Provence and Auvergne towers and then calculate the distance to the spot where Turkey would be," Gabe reasoned, feeling increasingly like he had to keep the peace between the other two by being the one who tried to move them forward rationally.

As they paced between the Castle towers, marking out the distances between countries and their equivalents here on the ground, Gabe allowed Dr. Gerard to get a little further ahead and fell into step with Saphy, for once sulky and pouty in a more insular way than her usual aggressive, forward manner. He was struggling to understand quite what it was that had got into her.

He knew that Saphy had not been comfortable around the fusty old buildings and traditions of Cambridge University. Her career as a student there had obviously not gone well and she had clearly been loath to return. Her relationship with Jane Cavendish had been one that had been nurturing for her spiky spirit, but Professor Cavendish had been an unconventional sort of Cambridge professor. Raymond Gerard, however, very much fit the stereotype that reminded Saphy of a world she would rather have left behind. However, Gabe wondered if, perhaps, there was something more to Saphy's sour mood.

Dr. Gerard's last remark had obviously hit home against something that made Saphy quite sensitive. She was used to being the dominant one in the growing relationship she had with Gabe. Intellectually she was very much in control and obviously appreciated being the one to provide him with all the knowledge her expensive education had given her, even while she derided that very education with her other moments. The presence of the even more knowledgeable and educated Dr. Gerard had stripped Saphy of her position as the brains of the operation and this had made her frustrated and irritable.

It was not just that Dr. Gerard's arrival changed Saphy's role in the quest to solve this mystery, the whole relationship between Gabe and Saphy had transformed with his becoming part of their adventure. In the few days that they had been together, Gabe and Saphy had both managed to bring something out of each other that they would never have achieved had they not been thrust into each other's company and had to work with each other and each other alone. The dynamic that they had built between them was really starting to work, a real connection was growing between them, but Dr. Gerard's presence made them revert right back to the way that they had been before. Still, Gabe was not completely sure if even that was enough to explain Saphy's mood.

"What are you getting so uptight about?" he half whispered as he walked beside her, "Aren't we getting close? Dr. Gerard can help us. What is your problem with him?"

"Doesn't it seem a little convenient?" Saphy asked, "Him just showing up like that, right here in the Castle, just at the moment we arrived."

"He was following the same clues we were," Gabe explained, "The same information in Robert White's research that led us here. Of course, if he was going to start in the same place at the same time and follow the same path then he would come to the same outcome as us at the same time. He obviously knows what he's doing. I think we could use his help."

"So, how did he know what we talked to Jane about?" she asked, "Nobody saw her again after we left her except for her killers."

"Well, I came to see him after we'd talked to Professor Cavendish," Gabe replied, "I told him that she'd told us about Hermaphroditus and Salmacis." "But not that we were interested in the Borghese statue. How did he know Jane had told us about that?" she asked again, "Look, we know we've been followed by both the naiads and these Hospitaller people, how do we know that Gerard arriving here isn't a part of that too?"

"So, if you suspect him of helping the people that are trying to kill us, why are you letting him stay and help us too?"

"I'd rather have him with us, where we can keep an eye on him, where we can make sure of what he's doing, than following us from the shadows," Saphy explained, "Besides, I might be wrong. I'm just saying to be on your guard."

"OK," Gabe agreed sceptically, distracted by the progress they were making towards the wall at the far end of the Castle, "Come on. I think he's found something."

Together, they quickened their pace and soon found themselves alongside Dr. Gerard in front of a section of the greystone wall. He was leaning in towards the stones, examining them closely, running his hands over the worn masonry. This was a corner of the Castle that was far from where the main towers stood and, therefore, away from the main tourist interests. The wall was rough and worn, covered in moss and lichen, which also grew on the flagstones of the surrounding floor. As they joined him, Dr. Gerard was brushing the moss away from a piece of stone to reveal a symbol scratched into it.

"Another sign that you've seen before, I think," he said as Gabe and Saphy leaned in to see the shape of a circle scratched into the stone, a circle with a cross beneath it and an arrow coming from the upper right hand side.

"The hermaphrodite symbol!" Gabe exclaimed excitedly, "Then we must be on the right track."

"Not necessarily," Saphy pointed out, "This stone, complete no doubt with its inscription, had been moved from its original position in the Mausoleum into the Castle during the 1522 reinforcement. Whatever it originally indicated could still be right up at the Mausoleum."

"I'm inclined to believe that the Hospitallers would have placed that specific stone in this specific spot for good reason," Dr. Gerard said.

He pushed against the symbol and the stone shifted a little in its mortar. There was a crumbling sound almost as if age old gears were turning behind the wall, giving a suggestion that the symbol was a button that could release a secret doorway into the ancient world. However, nothing happened, the wall did not open to reveal a passageway, it just stood still and inactive, bringing a feeling of intense disappointment into Gabe's mind.

"This stone is a trigger," Dr. Gerard said, "A release to bring the wall down and reveal something behind. However, there appears to be some other part to it, some further pressure needs to be applied elsewhere to make it work." "So, we just need to look around for something else to press," Saphy said, kneeling down against the wall and starting to clear away the dark green moss.

Pretty soon, between the three of them, they had uncovered the whole area of wall completely. All that they could do was stand back and stare at the complete blankness of it. Nothing new was revealed, no other buttons or triggers to be found at all. Gabe took a step back to look up at the whole extent of the wall and there was a metallic clunk as his shoe hit something that definitely was not a flagstone.

In a second, all three were on their knees, brushing away the green sludge that covered the small metallic plate that Gabe had stood on. It was not moss, it was some kind of rust or wear to the burnished brown metal. As they rubbed it away, the metal began to regain some of its sheen, beginning to reflect almost like a mirror. When pushed to put pressure on it, the metal plate shifted into the floor. Pressing the metal floor plate and the wall stone in unison, however, achieved no result at all.

"It's copper," Dr. Gerard said, "An odd choice for something left outside. Its glittering mirror surface is bound to become green before too long."

"Glittering... " Gabe turned the word over in his mind, it seemed to recall some earlier memory, "'Watch the world in glittering copper...'"

"What?" Saphy asked, "What does that mean?"

"Something...Something I saw in a dream," Gabe explained, "The mirror of the goddess, it said 'I would rather see the sparkle in your face than watch the world in glittering copper or see foot soldiers armoured in hard iron.'"

"The poet Sappho," Dr. Gerard recognised the words.

"Hmm, yes, although a bit of a misquote," Saphy agreed, "It seems that in your dream your subconscious mixed up all kinds of bits of information from the day."

"You don't know the half of it," Gabe admitted almost just into the air.

"What was that about the mirror of the goddess?" she asked.

"Glittering copper," he replied, "That was the mirror of Venus."

"Yes, that's true, why didn't we think of it before?" Dr. Gerard exclaimed, "The goddess Venus was always associated with the element of copper."

"Exactly," Saphy agreed, "You know, I completely forgot before when we were talking about the symbol when we first met, it seems like so long ago. One more thing that it represents is copper. You see that's why the circle with the cross beneath it. It's a mirror, Venus' symbol, the symbol of femininity and sexuality, just like in the painting. Mirrors were made of copper in ancient times."

"So, why is it here?" Gabe asked, "And why doesn't it open the door?" "Because it's only half of the system," she replied, "We've got our Venus. We just need Mars."

"What do you mean?"

"Remember what Jane said about the symbol on the wall there, about the significance of Hermaphroditus?" Saphy went on, "The ancient Greeks felt Hermaphroditus represented the ultimate union of male and female in one whole. It was a marriage symbol, the two halves united in one."

"Artemisia built the Mausoleum because she loved her husband so much, she wanted to become one with him," Gabe cottoned on, "She drank her husband's ashes to unite them in one body. That was why she revered Hermaphroditus."

"I see what you are suggesting," Dr. Gerard replied, "You think this plate here represents Venus and another represents Mars. Together, they will trigger the release."

"Mars? What represents Mars?" Gabe asked.

"Well, the Venus half is the copper mirror," Dr. Gerard explained, "The other half of the symbol, the circle with the arrow coming from the right side is Mars' shield and spear."

"Femininity is represented in the mirror, masculinity in the martial arms," Saphy added, as she walked over a few steps opposite where the copper plate lay, and started to feel around the flagstones, "Copper for girls and for boys..." she found the spot she was looking for and tapped her fist against it, the metal ringing out, "Iron."

"'Foot soldiers armoured in hard iron,'" Gabe quoted from his dream once more.

"Right, iron for boys," Saphy said, pulling Gabe over to stand on the iron plate, "So you stand here. Copper for girls, so I'll go over here," she stepped onto the copper plate, "And we'll see what happens when we do this."

Gabe felt the iron floor button give a little under his weight, felt it push down into the ground. A tingle of excitement ran through him as Saphy took him by the hand. Together they reached forward to push the loose masonry on the wall, their fingers interlocking together, their bodies moving as one, each reflecting the other. Gabe's heart pumped faster with the thrill as he heard a sound of stone becoming dislodged.

A couple of small pebbles tumbled from the top of the wall. Like the tiny stones that begin an avalanche, these pebbles were the beginning of something much bigger. Within a matter of seconds, the whole wall was tumbling down around them, meaning that Gabe and Saphy had to spring back from the metal pads on which they were standing to join Dr. Gerard behind a rock.

When the whole section of wall had collapsed in a flash of dirt and stone and the dust had settled, the three of them emerged to see what had stood behind, or rather beneath, it. The falling wall had revealed that it had once been built right across the entrance to a long, wide tunnel. Stone steps led down into the unknown darkness. Steps that had been covered for nearly five hundred years and now, finally, revealed.

"What is it?" asked Gabe staring down into the darkness of the newly discovered tunnel as they stood amongst the fallen stonework of the Castle wall, "Where does it lead?"

"I believe it is a ley tunnel," Dr. Gerard replied, "I've read and heard a lot about them, but never seen one for real."

"What's a ley tunnel?"

"Tunnels running along leylines, important lines of mystical significance, were a common feature amongst Templar architecture," he revealed, "They were used to hide the secrets of the Order. With many Templar secrets turning over to the Hospitallers, I guess we should not be surprised at them using the same techniques. Many ley tunnels linked strongholds like this Castle with other important locations."

"Like the Mausoleum," Saphy chipped in.

"Like the Fountain of Salmacis," Gabe added, excitedly.

"Well, I guess there's only one way to be sure," Dr. Gerard replied, stepping toward the dark and dusty tunnel steps.

"Come on, we're not getting left behind now, not when we're this close," Saphy said, grabbing Gabe by the arm as Dr. Gerard descended to the bottom of the steps.

The tunnel was filled with a filmy layer of dust, undisturbed for perhaps centuries. Gabe could feel it clogging up his lungs as he and Saphy descended the stone steps together to join Dr. Gerard. As they reached the bottom of the steps, they looked on ahead of them and could see nothing of where the tunnel headed, just pitch black. All three stood, hesitantly wondering which would be the first to step away from the last shaft of hot Turkish sunlight and enter the dark world of the unknown.

"Wait a second," Gabe suddenly said, "I've got a light."

He was still carrying his heavy bag full of camera equipment. He began to fish around in the bag until he pulled out a square flashlight that he sometimes attached to the camera to take photographs on dark days without having to use the camera's flash. Flicking the switch on the flashlight suddenly illuminated the dark, dusty tunnel before them. It was built with strong timber supports like a mine shaft, but so much older. The timber was thick and heavy, but worryingly rotten in places. Even with the beam of bright torchlight, it was difficult to see any end to the tunnel.

The light reassured the three of them a little, but even so, Gabe felt his heartbeat speed up with the first step that they took, all in unison, down the dark ancient tunnel. He had to fight strongly against a childish urge to reach out and hold onto Saphy's hand for reassurance. He got the feeling that this would not have been met by a similar response in his companion. For her part, Saphy, as ever, had a determined expression set on her face as she walked alongside him. The strong, harsh stare of Dr. Gerard, however, remained unreadable in the long shadows the tunnel cast across his face.

It was probably only a couple of minutes of walking silently side by side before they reached the end of the tunnel, but to Gabe it felt very much longer. It was hard to believe that up above them there was a modern Mediterranean beach resort, full of happy, relaxed tourists. Down here in ancient dark, it felt like time was completely unrelated to the world outside, that they had utterly left the 21st century behind and had entered a different dimension where time did not progress, and had not since the time of the old gods.

Now, however, they found themselves on the threshold of something new. The narrow, dark tunnel ended and they moved on into a larger chamber. While the tunnel had been dry and dusty, there was a sense of damp in the air of this room. All three could hear the sound of dripping water. Part of the chamber was illuminated by a beam of light coming not from Gabe's flashlight but from the Turkish sunshine in the world up above. As their eyes adjusted to the dark, Gabe, Saphy and Dr. Gerard began to take in what it was that the light shaft showed up.

Right in the middle of the room was a pool of stagnant water, obviously once built of elegant stone but now covered in dark green slime. On a ledge above the pool, there was a reclining classical statue in decaying bronze, illuminated by the beam of golden sunlight like the altar of some ancient temple.

Even in the dim light of the chamber, the figure was instantly recognisable to Gabe. It was one that he had been seeing a lot of recently, in reality, in paintings, even in his dreams. By now, he felt like he knew every inch of the figure's soft, sensual curves, from the little mounds of its breasts to the small penis nestling between its smooth thighs. Even with the years of decay, the statue's face retained that look of sensual yearning that had so entranced generations of poets and artists and even now captured Gabe's imagination.

"You don't think...That's not the original is it?" Saphy broke the silence, her educated diction hushed in awe.

Gabe barely heard her, however. He was so focused on what he was seeing, it was as if some other part of his mind had taken over and his usual conscious thought had been pushed out of the way. He did not even fully understand that the water that he saw before him could be the answer to what they had been looking for from the start. For him, it felt like an answer to a far older, deeper need within.

Later on, he would be completely unable to explain what he was thinking at that moment. He just knew that he had to do what he did. As soon as he saw that sludgy, stale water in the damp room, he was drawn in to it. Before Saphy and Dr. Gerard could really notice that there was something a little off about their companion, Gabe had let his heavy bag of camera equipment drop to the floor and had rushed across the room and plunged his whole body into the pool.

After years in this dark chamber, the water was freezing and the cold hit Gabe like a slap to the chest, knocking the breath completely out of him. For a moment, he was utterly disorientated with the dirty water in his eyes, filling his mouth with its dank taste. His mind was swirling wildly all over the place and he felt as if his body was no longer quite in his control, as if something strange was about to happen to it.

After a second, however, he surfaced, feeling cold, wet and dirty, but otherwise pretty much himself. Saphy had rushed over to the side of the pool and was leaning over to pull him out. She was staring at him with a curious expression on her face as if trying to figure out just what had been going through his mind.

"What the hell are you doing?" she asked incredulously.

"I don't know...I thought...Well, I don't really know what I thought," Gabe replied, starting to shiver from the cold, starting to feel pretty stupid.

"Well, stop being such a bloody fool and let's have a look around," Saphy told him, holding out her hand to help him out of the pool, "The statue must mean something, must mean that we're close. Although I guess we can see from you that the water's only magical transformation powers are to turn someone into a quivering idiot."

"Yeah," Gabe replied, wiping the slime off his shirt and stepping across the pool to climb out, "It was kind of stupid of me to think that there might really be something to it. That the water might really - ow!"

Gabe stopped mid-sentence, just as he was about to climb up out of the pool, and clutched at his foot. In the dark of the water, he had stood on something sharp and it had punctured his sneaker, pricking him on the foot.

"Damn it!" he cursed, "The floor here is really broken up and uneven. It's not easy to walk on."

Saphy let go of Gabe as he pulled himself up out of the water. She had brought over his camera bag and was now using the light to scan the bottom of the pool, looking at the sharp spot where Gabe had stood while he nursed the pain in his punctured foot.

"I don't think this is age," she said, "I think this is what it's supposed to be like. These peaks and dips, it's designed like that. There's something very familiar about these shapes."

"How do you mean?" said Gabe, his interest in his injured foot instantly switching to an interest in Saphy as she revealed her latest discovery, the latest clue in piecing the mystery together.

"Don't you think it kind of looks like a map?" she said, excitedly, "It's kind of a relief of an area of land. That point could be the peak of a mountain," she pointed out different areas with the flashlight, "This line could be the sea. That other bumpy bit there, that could be an island. And I'm sure it's one I recognise."

"That really is some smart observation. If only you would have remained at Cambridge, you could have made something of yourself," they had almost forgotten the presence of the middle aged academic and both were kind of surprised to have their usual deductions interrupted like this, "Mr. Herrison, I believe you have got yourself a good one there. Her suspicions are always so accurate."

There was something a little off in the manner that he said this, not like he was paying a compliment at all. There was an edge to his usual slightly superior manner that made Gabe and Saphy both look up with concern to see Dr. Gerard standing at the entrance to the chamber. He was not, however, alone. Two bright lights either side of the Cambridge academic revealed themselves as being flashlights attached to the handguns held by two men in black robes. On each robe, Gabe could see the white crosses that they had seen carved into the tower above them, the same he had seen in the cell back in Cambridge.

"What was it now that she said?" Dr. Gerard went on, "'Doesn't it seem a little convenient, showing up at the Castle right when you did?' Maybe you should have listened more to that thought. 'Be on your guard', I think she mentioned. Good advice, I would have thought."

There was an unpleasant note of triumph in his slightly foreign accent, "Don't you realise that the sole reason that you are still alive is because I have allowed you to be?"

"I don't understand," Gabe replied.

"In Cambridge, I had to ensure that those two eunuch assassins did not kill you as they had Jane Cavendish. You should be grateful to me for that, it took all my power to do it. After that, you two proved yourselves quite the little code crackers. I decided that we would be better off using your skills rather than keeping you out of the way. And you certainly have more than lived up to our hopes for you."

"In Cambridge? But, you're a university professor. How do you have the power to call off assassins? Who are you?"

"They're Hospitallers," Saphy responded, "Or at least, they like to think that they are."

"The Priory of Villeneuve represents the original ideals of the Order of the Knights Hospitaller," Dr. Gerard replied with a note of anger and aggression in his voice, "We seek to heal the ills of the world, to bring order and righteous Christian morality. By any means necessary. The Knights Hospitaller in their glory days had access to this weapon of incredible power and they were too scared to use it. They hid it away beneath their stronghold, but now we have the power to set that right."

"The Fountain of Salmacis is a weapon?" Gabe asked, feeling strangely disturbed by the idea.

"Think about it, the ability to reduce the mightiest of your enemies to a weak and feeble woman," Dr. Gerard replied.

"Weak and feeble woman?!" Saphy sprang forward angrily, "I'll show you a fucking weak and feeble woman."

She was quickly brought to a halt however as the two robed men stepped forward and gestured significantly with their pistols. Seeing this, Saphy came to her senses and took a step back, even whilst her posture remained defiant, glaring with her fierce, piercing eyes at the Cambridge academic and secret Grand Prior of a mediaeval holy order.

"We have allowed you to live thus far, Miss Cross, make sure that you don't seem to outlive your usefulness," Dr. Gerard said, carefully pronouncing each word as if to leave no doubt as to the nature of his threat, "Robert White was very useful to us at first, but in the end he proved a liability."

"Wait! It was you?" Gabe exclaimed, shocked to have one of the many mysteries that they sought to uncover resolved so simply and bluntly, "You knew all along where White was, what had become of him. You knew because it was you that killed him!"

"I'm afraid not. We did not kill Professor White," Dr. Gerard replied, "Robert had been my mentor many years ago and I was reluctant to make that final necessary decision, once we had gained all we could from him. Fortunately, that decision was taken out of my hands. Yes, I do know just what happened to Professor White. You see -"

However, Dr. Gerard had no chance to finish his sentence. He was interrupted just at the moment when both Gabe and Saphy were just coming to listen intently to all he was about to reveal them. As the crucial words were just about to leave his lips, just at that very moment, he span round in surprise to see the hooded black figure behind him slump to the ground. A white feathered arrow was embedded in his back. Gabe, sitting on the floor beside the pool, watched as Saphy dived to the ground just as a second arrow whizzed threw the air and embedded itself in the timber roof support just beyond where she had been standing. She flattened herself low against the ground and began to inch her way, slithering dignity free across the dirt, slowly and methodically, seeking the small amount of shelter offered by the stone wall around the pool, the same wall behind which Gabe had just ducked.

The second black robed Hospitaller took one look at his comrade, impaled by the arrow, and put his back to the wall to the right of the narrow tunnel that was the only way in or out of the chamber. Another arrow whistled through the air towards the commanding figure of the Grand Prior, Raymond Gerard. Gabe was certain that he was about to see the man he had previously viewed as an ageing academic stuck with a sharp shaft penetrating his flesh. However, the moment that the arrow hit the spot where Gerard had been standing, he was no longer there. Following the example set by his guard, Gerard had backed himself against the wall.

Peering out from behind the wall, Gabe watched as Gerard drew a pistol from his jacket pocket. In unison, Gerard and the other Hospitaller spun around to face the narrow tunnel and fired three shots each, lighting up the dark, dusty walkway with flashes and flares. Here, in the quiet deep beneath the town, undisturbed in generations, each gunshot shook right through Gabe's body. He was starting to breathe heavily, he felt the blood rush to his ears as everything seemed blurred and confusing like film slowed down with the sound on mute.

He looked across at Saphy, hiding, her back against the low wall of the pool. Even in the haze of his vision, Gabe could see her eyes widened and her chest rising and falling with sharp, excitable breaths. While he slumped against the wall, just praying for it to be over, she was alert, her eyes darting around the darkened chamber for anything that could be a way out for them. They made quite a pair, cowering in the dirt, him covered in mucky water from the pool, her with muddy slime down her front from slithering across the floor.

After the quick burst of flashes and ear splitting noise that came from both men's handguns, there was a temporary silent respite in which Gabe tried to follow Saphy's example, get his head together and look for a way out. Meanwhile, Gerard gesticulated from his companion to the tunnel down which they had just fired, indicating that the reluctant Hospitaller should be the one to ensure that their blind shots had hit their target.

Glancing around awkwardly, the black robed figure stepped out from his position against the wall and directed the beam of his flashlight down the dusty tunnel. As Gerard remained out of harm's way, the other man took a few ginger steps down the tunnel until the light he was shining was swallowed up by the dark. Gabe looked from the tunnel to Saphy and back again during the agonising few seconds of silent waiting, unsure which he would rather see, that black robe emerging from the tunnel once again, ready to turn his killer attention back on them, or nobody to return and him and Saphy left to become a pin cushion for the naiads' white feathered arrows.

Suddenly, the silence was broken by another flash of gunfire and a muffled cry. A second later, the Hospitaller staggered back into the chamber, his gun clattered to the floor as he stumbled backwards. His other hand clutched at his chest. Thick, dark crimson blood welled up on his lips. His hand flailed around but failed to do anything about the arrow shaft that pierced his lung. Finally, his legs gave out and he collapsed onto the floor, his head just inches from the pool that Gabe and Saphy were using as a hiding place.

He was still breathing, but with the arrow stuck inside him he was coughing up bubbles of blood. Even though this man was about to kill him a few minutes earlier, Gabe struggled to watch his slow and painful death. It reminded him so much of the first person he had seen shot with one of those arrows, the woman at the National Gallery.

Gabe had no more time to contemplate the body, however, as he felt Saphy grab his hand and pull him to his feet. He looked across at where the Hospitaller had stumbled back and saw Gerard discharge the rest of his pistol wildly around the entrance to the tunnel. A white dressed figure took a shot to the chest and slumped into the room, but she was swiftly followed by another. This second naiad dropped her bow and pulled from her quiver full of arrows a long, slender knife and turned on the erstwhile classics professor.

"Come on," Saphy hissed as she pulled Gabe against the wall of the dark chamber, keeping them in the shadows, "Don't look."

He noticed that for all her decisive conduct, she kept her eyes turned away from the spluttering body of the dying Hospitaller. She too, it seemed, could not get the image of the first victim from her mind. However, she was focusing her energies and attention instead on getting well away from it, and the possibility of the same thing happening to them.

Gerard had the naiad grabbed by the wrist as they struggled over her knife. His wasted pistol dropped to the floor with the one his companion had let fall as he collapsed to the ground. Locked as they were in this struggle, neither noticed the movement in the shadows at the edge of the chamber, the two shapes that inched along the wall toward the tunnel that would lead them back to daylight and, just perhaps, to make their escape.

CHAPTER 3

Gabe's heart beat a rapid, irregular pace. His hand grasped Saphy's with unashamed panic. He felt no distress at putting himself entirely in her control, he just wanted her to get them out of this. She, for once, offered no resistance to the intimacy of this childlike pressing together of their sweaty skin in the dark moment. Over his other arm, he had slung the camera bag, another security blanket in his moment of panic. It weighed heavily on his shoulder and thumped against his thigh, but he did nothing to cast it aside or drop it.

Their progress to the entrance to the chamber was painfully slow, worried that either of the two figures struggling in the centre of the room would catch their escape, but as they neared the dusty tunnel, Saphy began to pick up the pace, starting to tug at Gabe's hand, to pull him on and away. He, however, was experiencing a certain reluctance to leave the pool and statue behind. He knew the desperation of their situation, but that beautiful, androgynous reclining figure and that stagnant water represented their one last and best chance at uncovering the mystery, at finally making their way to the transformative fountain of his dreams.

Nevertheless, he could not ignore the more immediate danger. And so, with one final regretful glance at the statue in that pose that started it all, he allowed Saphy to tug him into the tunnel. Now, away from the sight lines of Gerard and the naiad, they quickened their pace until they broke into a run, making their way back through the dusty dark so much quicker than they had come the other way.

Daylight raced towards them as a hand grasped at Saphy's flailing ankle. It was another woman dressed in a white tunic, only this tunic was quickly turning dark red. There were bullet wounds in her stomach and shoulder. Barely glancing down, Saphy broke her step only to stamp hard and brutally down on the grasping hand and keep running, never looking back to see what damage she had done, just desperate to get out of there. Her hand, still held in Gabe's felt warm and sweaty.

Their lungs filled with fresh air as they felt the heat of the Turkish sun hit them with a blast at the bottom of the stone steps. They paused for a moment to take a breath of it. They had been gasping at centuries old dust and dirt down there and real air felt so good in their exhausted, panicked throats. Then, hand in hand, they bounded up the steps two at a time. They were so close to being back in the castle, back in Bodrum the tourist seaside town where murder and mythology seemed so far from people's minds.

Gabe and Saphy emerged, blinking and dazzled into the sunshine. They took a moment to catch their breath and exchanged looks of relief and silly pleasure to be away from the dark. Saphy's clothing, already ripped and held together with safety pins, was even more torn up and covered in slimy dirt. Her flame red hair was an utter mess and there was a streak of mud running across her left cheek. Still, she had a glow of life that made her, to Gabe's eyes, seem genuinely attractive in a way he had never quite thought of before. He could only imagine how he must look, still dripping wet from the dirty, ancient water.

After a moment, they realised that they were still holding hands. Both blushed in unison and quickly withdrew them, unsure of quite what to say. Gabe turned his gaze away, not wanting to look Saphy in the eye, and caught sight of a shadow falling across the sun. He turned back to mention it to Saphy. Too late, however, strong, long arms already held her in a firm grip.

In seconds, the twin of those arms grabbed his chest so tight it took the breath right out of him. Odd looking shaven heads, no less sinister for their increasing familiarity, loomed above them. Saphy struggled against the grip, stamped her feet, but the assassin holding her had seen this technique from her before. He lifted her an inch or two from the ground and held her around her waist, so her arms were pinned to her side. All she could do was flail and kick at air and, eventually, she seemed to realise the futility of it. Gabe, for his part, was near paralysed with fear of what was to come.

"You should know, sinners, you cannot escape us," hissed the assassin, Phobus or possibly Deimus, that held Saphy, "You may flee, you may hide, but wherever you go, fear and dread will always find you eventually."

"Soon, however, your nightmare will be over," the other said in his high pitched lisping sigh, "We will purify this world of you."

"Now, now, there'll be a time for that soon enough," came the voice of Raymond Gerard, now emerging from the ley tunnel beneath the castle, "We may need them yet. But I have perhaps found a better solution that could lead us even quicker to our end."

As he appeared over the top of the steps and out of the collapsed wall around the tunnel, it became clear that he too was escorting a captive. The naiad that he had been struggling with was now held by his grip in one hand, with the other holding her own long knife to her throat. She looked young and pretty, younger than Saphy, with long, dark curls. She was less tall, strong and imposing than Atalanta, the other naiad Gabe had seen properly, but she retained a look of stern defiance in the face of her capture.

Gabe wished that he could mirror that look, but he knew he felt real panic. He knew now that his life and Saphy's were only valuable while Gerard and the Hospitallers thought they could be of assistance. If they could extract the information they needed from the naiad, then the rest of their lives could be very short indeed.

It was at least a larger, roomier, airier cell than the one in which they had locked him back in Cambridge. Other than that, however, this situation had a distressing sense of familiarity to Gabe. This time he had not blacked out when assaulted by the bald eunuch assassins, but he had been far too fearful and panicked to notice especially where they were being taken. All that he knew was that they were still in Bodrum, they had not been moved that far. The Hospitallers must have a base of operations designed to be close by their original castle.

This time, of course, there was also the difference that he was not alone. The room had probably once served as a wine cellar. It was long and thin with a vaulted ceiling. However, one side of the room had been converted into a series of cage like cells made up of iron bars and locked gates. Gabe sat on a hard wooden bench in one of these cells. In the next one along, Saphy was pacing back and forth, separated from Gabe by just a set of bars. Next to her, the naiad sat in the centre of the floor, unmoving, staring defiantly out. In the other half of the room, there were a pair of guards in the black Hospitaller robes.

There were a lot of these guards around. The whole operation here seemed a lot more efficient and organised than it had in Cambridge. They had been subject to a pretty exhaustive search when they had been brought in here. They had been stripped and dressed in shapeless white smocks that covered most of their bodies in one piece of material. Gabe's ubiquitous bag of camera equipment now lay in the corner of the room, unreachable on the other side of the bars. A little nearer, but still beyond grasp of their hands, there was a pile of their clothes.

Gabe watched as Saphy paced, his own slumped despairing posture was the complete opposite to her fidgety inability to remain still for a moment. In the third cell, the naiad was as unmoving as Gabe, but her face had an expression of calm that he could not feel. He could see no way out now and knew that as soon as the Hospitallers and Gerard could extract what they needed to know from the naiad then he and Saphy would rapidly become surplus to the warrior monks' requirements.

Saphy seemed lost in her own thoughts, trying desperately to figure something out. Her eyes mostly remained fixed to the floor as she paced like a caged zoo animal, always following the same track. Gabe could feel the eyes of the guards on him, though, even from behind the black shadow of their hooded robes. It made him feel uncomfortable about even moving. He felt very exposed, trapped and watched. For a moment, he wondered how the subjects of his photographs felt, knowing he was always there watching from behind his camera. He didn't much like the thought.

Footsteps sounded on the stairs leading down to the cellar. There was a certain degree of urgency to the sound that made Gabe's heart jump with fear. Saphy stopped pacing and looked up, catching Gabe's eye. She had a look of steely determination and, last week, that was all that Gabe would have noticed in her look. Now, however, he could see beyond that, could see the fear that was in his eyes mirrored back in hers. She opened her mouth to speak, but was silenced instantly by an angry word from the guard.

The door to the cellar flew open and in strode Dr. Gerard, the Grand Prior, flanked by two of his robed henchmen. All three were dressed in the order's black robes with white crosses, but their hoods were down to reveal their faces. Looking up, Gabe realised that the two men accompanying Gerard were equally familiar. It was DI Gilbert and DS Godfrey from the Cambridge Police Force. Gilbert gave him a nasty looking smirk. Godfrey, meanwhile focused his attention on the beautiful naiad in the third cell.

"We'll deal with you later," Gerard dismissively turned from Gabe and Saphy and walked quickly over to the cell where the naiad was being held, "You, however, can tell us just what we need to know right now," he said to her, then to the guards, "Unlock this cell and bring her with me."

Godfrey opened the door of the cell and walked over to where the naiad sat silently on the bench. He laid his hand on the small young woman's shoulder, but, before anyone in the room had time really to comprehend what was happening, he doubled over in pain. The naiad's hand had moved at incredible speed and struck the detective hard in his solar plexus. In a second, she had sprung up, swinging on the bars of the cell, her leg spun and landed a hard kick to the side of Godfrey's head, bringing him to the floor.

He struggled to get to his feet and, in doing so, swung his fist wildly at the spot where she had been standing. She was simply too fast for him ever to make use of his superior size and strength. Before he could stand, she was on top of him, her hands wrapped around his head.

With a sickening crack that made Gabe gasp out loud, she twisted his head in her hands, snapping his neck, and dropping his limp body to the floor.

"Impressive," came the sound of Gerard's sneering, superior voice as he clapped his hands together, "But completely useless."

Gabe turned his attention from the naiad and saw that the other three Hospitallers had now approached. All had drawn their guns. The naiad looked around for a way out but found none and was soon taken by both arms by the two hooded guards that had been standing by the door.

"You can kill me if you will, I will never reveal the secrets of my sisterhood," she spat out defiantly.

"Oh I won't kill you," Gerard replied, "Not yet, anyway. I've got something much better in store for you. Well, better for me, worse for you."

He led the way as the two guards escorted the naiad from the room. Gilbert stood behind, staring at his police partner with shocked awe.

"Get rid of that body," Gerard said, turning back to him before leaving the cellar.

Gilbert glared angrily at Saphy and Gabe as he dragged his partner's heavy corpse from the room, never saying anything but conveying quite clearly in his eyes the feeling of hate he had toward them, hate and blame for what he had just witnessed the naiad do. He slammed the door behind him and the sound of him angrily dragging his partner's body continued for some time.

Gabe and Saphy, locked in their adjoining cells, were left alone in the cellar. For a few moments they stayed in complete silence, just trying to absorb what had just happened. Saphy was no longer pacing, she just stared across the cellar, unspeaking.

"She'll be OK," Gabe said, just wanting to break the silence, "She can handle herself."

Finally, Saphy turned to face him, but what she said next did not appear to follow on at all from what he had said, nor what had just happened.

"Back in the cave," she began to say, to Gabe's surprise, "Why the hell did you dive into that pool of dirty slime like that?"

"Honestly? I have no idea," Gabe replied, "I just felt compelled to do it, like I really needed to feel it."

"What were you hoping to get out of it?" Saphy questioned.

"I...I just needed to do it. I can't answer more than that. I wasn't really thinking rationally."

"Because, to my mind there's only two possible outcomes," Saphy had come right up to the bars separating their two cells now, turning her smart, sharp gaze thoughtfully on him, "Either this really was the mythological Fountain of Salmacis and, by diving in, you would become a woman, or it's just an old puddle of stagnant water and, by diving in, you'd have got wet, cold and dirty. So, why would you want either?"

"Like I said, I didn't think about what I wanted."

"Even so, there must have been an instinct inside you that made that choice. Given that I can't believe you wanted a dunking in sludgy water, I can only conclude that, at least in part, you wanted to see if the myth was true. You wanted the waters to make you a woman!"

"Don't be ridiculous," Gabe said defensively, "I just...I needed to know if it was true. You're right about that part at least."

"But why?" Saphy pondered before continuing her train of thought to answer the question before he could articulate it himself, "That story has always fascinated you, hasn't it? You grew up wondering whether it could possibly be real."

"Yes, exactly," Gabe agreed, surprised at how well she had come to know his inner thoughts, "How could you know that?"

"I've seen how you responded to Jane Cavendish introducing the idea of Hermaphroditus, how you behaved on seeing the statue at the Louvre. You're a stay at home introvert and yet you've been whisked away on this adventure, caught up in it because you feel you may finally come close to just what you've dreamed of all these years."

In all his life, Gabe had never met anyone who really understood how he felt. Ever since his first fascination with Love's Children and the Hermaphroditus story, he had never felt anybody else could grasp what it meant to him. But here was Saphy, this strange, aggressive, troubled intellectual, a woman whose life was so far from his own, telling him just how he felt.

Saphy still stood right by the bars of the cell, leaning in to talk to him in a breathy, excited voice that he had not heard her use before. He was drawn towards her now as he had been to the pool in the cave. He found himself standing close to the bars on his side of the cage until they were face to face, so close to each other that they were almost touching.

"But it isn't just a burning curiosity to see if the reality behind the myth, is it?" she went on, "Whatever you say, you want it to be true. You want to be able to plunge into the cold waters of the fountain and emerge with a beautiful body. A body you feel comfortable in. All these years you have never felt happy in your own body, you've longed to challenge and change it. You want to transform, like a butterfly, into something beautiful. I know you Gabe, I know what you're feeling. And I know that you do really want to become a woman as beautiful as Salmacis, as Venus, as Hermaphroditus."

"Yes," Gabe sighed, finally realising for himself that she was right, that part of his fascination with the

Fountain of Salmacis was a yearning to transform himself completely, "If only I could, if only it were true."

Her eyes fixed on his, staring deeply into his soul until all each could see was each other's eyes.

And then she kissed him.

He was shocked. Even in this moment of shared intimacy, he had not expected this. And yet here it was. The imposing, aggressive lesbian who had quarrelled and teased him now had her lips pressed wetly against his through the bars of the cage. Her tongue slid over his, her tongue stud rubbing against his mouth.

Everything else in the room faded out completely, he was lost in Saphy's long, lingering kiss. The cells seemed to disappear around them and it seemed to Gabe that, as the kiss continued, he was standing in soft grass beneath the hot sun, that he heard running water.

Sure enough, as he looked beyond Saphy's face, still pressing their lips together, he could see a stream of clear running water and out of it, emerging just like the image on the cover of Love's Children, was a familiar figure of incredible beauty, her naked body draped with long golden hair. Venus.

"Now is the time my son," she said in a soft whisper that made Gabe wonder if Saphy could here it too, "Now is the time to become the real you."

Suddenly, the vision disappeared to be replaced with the harsh environment of the cellar and the cell bars as

Saphy broke from their deep kiss. It seemed clear then to Gabe that the divine manifestation of the love goddess had only been for him, perhaps only ever in his head. Still, something had caught Saphy's attention to make her pull away so suddenly with such an exclamation.

"Of course!" she cried, as soon as her mouth was hers again, "Our clothes, that's it. We're getting the fuck out of here."

"Huh?" Gabe was confused, clearly no longer sharing her thoughts, "How are our clothes going to get us out? And, anyway, they're way over there. How do we get at them?"

"Just watch," Saphy smirked.

With no further words, she had pulled the white smock she was wearing right over her head, completely exposing her naked body to Gabe's view. He knew that the polite thing to do would be to turn away, but after the depth of passion in that kiss he felt no shame in seeing Saphy completely unclothed, seeing her whole story spelt out in the tattoos that covered her skin.

While Gabe stared at her open mouthed, Saphy was not idle. She twisted the shapeless material into a sort of a rope and flung it between the bars of the cage where it flopped down on the cellar floor and Saphy pulled it back in like a fisherman without a catch.

Seeing this, Gabe cottoned on to just what was happening. Saphy was trying to use the makeshift rope to pull their clothes from the pile across the cell back toward them. He had no idea how this was going to get them out or what possible benefit it could have beyond giving them something more usual to wear. Still, he had come to trust Saphy's brain and was willing to support what she did without knowing why she did it.

"Here," he said, turning to take the bundle of Saphy's clothes from her, unable to help himself eyeing up the curve of her breasts and between her legs, "Let me have a go. I'm closer."

Saphy handed him the crudely constructed rope and he had two or three goes at throwing the end across the room before, finally, making it land squarely in the pile of clothes across the cellar. It caught against something on Saphy's baggy, torn punk t-shirt. This was the only thing he could pull from the pile, but Saphy seemed excited and reached between the bars of her cell and grabbed it just as it slipped from the rope Gabe was pulling in.

She quickly pulled the large t-shirt over her head, covering her breasts and much of her nakedness, while her pale thin legs remained exposed. Her tattooed chest now hid behind the aggressive image of the punk logo emblazoned across her shirt. The tears in the material allowed glimpses of her skin beneath as safety pins did little to hold them together. It was one of these pins that Saphy now unfastened.

"See, all along I've been prepared for just such an eventuality as this," she grinned, "Because I've been walking around wearing a complete set of fucking first class lock picks."

Gabe watched, impressed, as Saphy took the point of two safety pins and inserted them into her cell's lock, feeling her way for a point that would give.

"Are you sure this will work?" he wondered.

"Don't worry," she grinned, excited to be problem solving once more, "This isn't the first time I've done this."

Sure enough, Gabe heard a click and, in seconds, the door to Saphy's cell swung open. Moments later, he too stood outside the cell, watching as Saphy pulled her mini-skirt and biker boots back on. She was now starting to look more like herself again.

For his part, Gabe remained dressed in the white smock the jailers had put him in. His concern was not for his clothes but for the camera equipment that he had carried with him all the way from England. He opened the bag and started eagerly looking over all his equipment, making sure that it was still all operational.

"What the hell are you doing?" Saphy demanded impatiently, "Get dressed and then let's get the fuck out of here. We need to plan our next move." "That's just what I'm doing," Gabe answered, "We're still headed for the Fountain, right? They're not going to stop us now."

"Hell no, they're not."

"Right," he agreed, "So, we need a clue. We need to remember what was in that pool in the cave."

"The map?" she sighed, "It really looked familiar. If only we could remember it. I don't much fancy going back to the castle. Gerard's sure to have it watched even if we can get past the guards to get out of here."

"Good thing I have a photographic memory," Gabe smirked, "And I mean that in a very literal sense."

He held up his camera, he was scrolling through pictures on the viewing screen.

"You remember the underwater photography equipment I've been carrying?" he smiled, "I know you thought it was a heavy inconvenience, but let's just treat this as my version of your lock picks." "You mean...?"

"That's right, while you were distracted talking to Gerard, I used this to get a shot under the pool. It's kind of blurry but you can certainly make out the map."

Eagerly, she came over and peered over his shoulder at the small screen. Sure enough, it showed a hastily taken image beneath the murky waters in the cave at Bodrum Castle. It was not quite straight, nor completely in focus, but the shape of what appeared to be an island, a coastline and a mountain were obvious.

"I know that island," Saphy exclaimed, "That's why it's familiar. It's Lesbos."

"Lesbos?"

"It's Sappho's home island," she said, "Sappho the subject of the Swinburne poetry, the lesbian icon, the one who I take my name from, just like lesbians take theirs from the island."

"So, what's Sappho got to do with the Fountain?"

"Where was Hermaphroditus from? In your story book, I mean."

"Mount something," he could not quite remember. "Mount Ida?"

"That's it. Why?"

"Because Lesbos is an island in a bay just off the coast of Turkey. The mountain that stands above that bay, the one on the map, is a mountain called Kazdagi, or Goose Mountain, but, historically, it used to be called Mount Ida."

"That's it then!" Gabe said, excitedly, "That must be where this quest ends. There, on the mountain, where the map shows the sign of that stream," he pointed, "That must be where to find the real Fountain of Salmacis!"

"What are we waiting for then?" Saphy looked bold and decisive, "Let's get out of here before they find we're gone."

Both turned toward the door of the cellar and, at that exact moment, heard the sound of footsteps in the corridor outside and looked in fear to see the door handle begin to turn.

Gabe froze as the door to the cellar began to open. Saphy slammed herself back against the wall on the side of the door that was beginning to open. She motioned dramatically at Gabe for him to do the same, a frown on her face beneath the flame coloured hair. As the entrance to the room opened, all Gabe could do was try and conceal himself behind the swinging door.

There were two of the Hospitaller guards dressed in the black robes with white crosses, both with hoods up. The first guard stepped into the room and saw the open, empty cells and gave out a startled grunt. Turning round, he instantly spotted Saphy backed against the wall.

However, in doing so he turned his back completely on Gabe, seeming to forget that there were supposed to be two people in the room. Grasping the first heavy thing to hand, the camera he still held, Gabe's only thought was to hit the guard as hard as he possibly could, to knock him down in one go.

Raising the camera above his head, he swung with his full strength, bringing the weight of the camera down on the unsuspecting skull of the hooded guard. There was a sickening crunch, a crack in both head and camera, and the guard slumped at Gabe's feet.

Just at that moment, the second guard crossed the threshold to see his partner lying prone on the cellar floor. He looked up with surprise, but the split second he had spent processing what might have happened to his companion was enough for Saphy, desperate and violent, to seize the advantage.

Wearing her biker boots once more, she stamped down hard on his foot causing him to stagger forward. Not allowing him the chance to regain his balance, she planted her sharp knee right into his groin causing him to double over with pain. Gabe now jumped in, bringing the now split open camera down on a second head. Another crunch, another thud, and the second guard sprawled out next to the first.

Gabe looked down in disappointment at his broken camera. It had got them this far, had helped them solve a few clues. But, more importantly, it had always been how he defined himself, something to cling onto, something to hide behind.

"Never mind that now," Saphy said, "We've got to get out of here. Help me get these guards into the cells. Take off their robes."

With one last look at his shattered camera, Gabe cast it aside. After that kiss, he felt like a different person anyway, felt like a new start. Perhaps he didn't need the camera's safety blanket quality any more.

It took a while to drag the heavy bodies of the Hospitaller guards across the cellar, but they were fortunate in that the Hospitallers in the rest of the building seemed happy that those two guards would be enough to look after their less capable prisoners and, therefore, nobody came to check on them.

Finally, they were able to leave the two of them in their cells and Saphy did her best job of locking them in. Gabe and Saphy were now dressed in the Hospitaller robes, Gabe still in his white prisoner smock underneath, Saphy in her biker boots poking out of the bottom of the robe.

"Keep your hood up," said Saphy, raising hers to hide her bright red hair, "And we should fit in. All we need to do then is walk steadily and calmly until we find a way out. Do nothing to attract attention and we'll be fine."

With their black hoods raised, everything around seemed darker and harder to see. Gabe could understand now why the guards had not immediately noticed them when they had walked into the cellar, the hoods may have been good for anonymity but they clearly weren't designed for good peripheral vision. He decided just to focus on what was in front of him and keep walking.

Above the cellar the building was a maze of identical grey corridors. Picking a likely route, or at least one that was as likely as any other, Saphy set out along one of these and Gabe followed close behind. Occasionally, they would pass other figures in black robes, their faces covered by cowls just like Saphy and Gabe. The Hospitallers asked no questions and Saphy and Gabe were only too pleased not to have to respond.

After what was, in reality, a few minutes, but felt like plenty more, it appeared they were going nowhere. They continued to pass identical looking dark wood doors that hid who knows what secrets. But, finally, what appeared to be an exit came into sight, a large set of double doors with a push bar. Both Saphy and Gabe could sense that beyond that door lay the city of Bodrum and their chance for escape. Before they could get to it, however, there was a room where one of the doors was slightly ajar.

"Do not assume we will not have our ways of extracting whatever information we desire from you," the familiar creeping voice of Raymond Gerard, the Grand Prior, drifted from the room. This is what they would have to pass to reach the exit.

Saphy made a move to slip quietly past the semi-ajar doorway, but Gabe could not help but let his curiosity take over. If Gerard was about to learn some answers from the naiad then he wanted to hear them too. Against his better judgement, and Saphy's angry gesticulating, Gabe moved closer to the doorway, peering through into the room beyond, listening in on what was happening within.

The room was small and dark with the naiad, still dressed in the same sort of smock that Gabe was wearing beneath his robe, strapped to a sort of angled metal table in the middle of the room under the only light source, a bright spotlight, her ankles and wrists were tied to the corners of the table. She was flanked either side by the two tall bald assassins, Phobus and Deimus along with one other hooded Hospitaller guard. The only other person in the room was Gerard, who, Gabe noticed, had a cut across his forehead. Obviously the naiad had not submitted to being tied down without putting up a fight.

"We took this from our erstwhile colleague, Professor White," he was explaining, his hand on an ivory miniature of the Borghese Hermaphroditus sculpture, it was a container for some sort of liquid, "He found out about this in the diaries of John Evelyn, reputedly it contains the actual waters of the Fountain of Salmacis," the naiad remained stubbornly silent, "That is to say that baptising somebody in these waters should turn them female. Why don't we put it to the test?"

Gerard summoned the guard forward. He stepped up somewhat reluctantly, removing his hood. It was Detective Inspector Gilbert, the supposed Cambridge policeman and secret Hospitaller. His partner in crime had already been disposed of and now he seemed nervous about what was about to be done to him.

Gerard poured the waters of the miniature sculpture over Gilbert's head as if baptising him. The clear waters ran down the police inspector's face and Gabe's heart skipped a beat in excited anticipation. Perhaps now he was finally about to see the true effects of the Fountain. Perhaps it did really work!

He waited excitedly and watched as nothing at all happened. Gilbert looked relieved to be still in his previous, male body, albeit slightly wetter. Gerard looked at him with a look that conveyed a certain amount of contempt, but appeared completely unsurprised by the lack of an outcome. Presumably this was not the first time he had tried this experiment. The twin assassins did not look much impressed either. Gabe began to wonder how far they were really supporting the abomination against nature that they must perceive the Fountain's supposed magical powers.

"Nothing," Gerard returned his attention to the defiant, silent naiad, "And yet we know that Professor White found it much more instructive. What, may I ask, is the secret White knew that we did not? That is all I want from you my pretty little thing."

"No," she said in a quiet but determined voice, the first words she had uttered, "I will never give up the secrets of my sisterhood. Each naiad would rather die than tell these."

"There are worse things a man can do to an innocent like you than to kill you," Gerard sneered.

Gabe stopped listening here as Saphy grabbed his arm angrily and pulled him against the wall.

"What the hell do you think you're doing?" she hissed, "We need to leave. Now."

"We can't just leave," Gabe replied, "We have to do something."

"Do something?"

"We have to stop them. To rescue her. We can't let the Hospitallers do whatever they want with her."

"Yeah, 'cause she'd do everything she could to rescue us if the tables were turned," Saphy interjected sarcastically, "Going in there is a surefire way to get us all captured and, quite probably, killed. I didn't go through all that bloody effort to get out of the cell just to end up back there."

For a moment, Gabe looked back into the interrogation room.

"You see, my pretty thing, you naiads do not fear death," Gerard was saying as he loomed over her, "We know this. But it does not make you fearless. You fear violation. Violation of your oaths, of your pure body. That is what we will give you unless you provide us with our answers."

The naiad's previously composed expression had now switched to one of wide eyed fear, but she kept resolutely quiet on providing the information Gerard sought.

Gerard tore her smock apart with a violent action until her near naked body was just draped in shreds of ripped fabric. He leered unpleasantly at her and began to open his own robe, unbuttoning the pants beneath as she began to struggle against her bonds.

"This is not what we agreed," the angry voice of one of the bald eunuchs came in.

"This is a disgrace to your cause and to us," the other added.

"Leave us then," Gerard growled back at them, "I am done with you. You have no understanding of what needs to be done to achieve real power."

He laughed menacingly and positioned himself between the innocent naiad's naked legs as his two hired assassins strode toward the door where Saphy and Gabe stood outside.

"Come on," Gabe grabbed her arm, "We have to help."

"We have to leave," Saphy countered.

"They're going to rape her!" he said urgently.

"I'm going to regret this," Saphy sighed, before bursting through the door of the interrogation room, "Stop now and we'll show you the way right to the Fountain," she said to Gerard as he hideously pushed himself between the naiad's thighs.

"Ha," he laughed, "No need if it doesn't work. I'll get just what I want from this one."

Gabe rushed into the room to join Saphy but, as he did so, everything became truly chaotic. Without caring what they did, Phobus and Deimus, the tall, strong bald killers strode past and slammed Gabe and Saphy back into the walls, not looking back to finish the job. Both walked into the corridor. Gabe and Saphy were painfully winded and bruised as they hit the wall, but otherwise fine.

Saphy staggered to her feet watching in horror as the Grand Prior did as he wished with the naiad. She stumbled forward, determined to stop him. Despite his pain, Gabe knew that he had to be there with her. Clawing himself to his feet, he followed Saphy's lead.

"Get them, Gilbert," the Grand Prior screamed, not turning from his vicious purpose, "Kill them."

On this command, Gilbert stepped toward Saphy, prepared to strike her down, prepared to revenge himself for all that Gabe and Saphy had done as well as the naiad's killing of his partner. Still Saphy staggered forward, but she never made it.

An oddly familiar sound was heard as something too fast to be seen zipped through the air. Gilbert stopped in his tracks, he coughed and blood flowed from his lips. Looking down in shock he saw an arrow stuck from his chest, where it was shortly joined by another. He staggered one more step and then collapsed in front of a surprised Saphy.

Both Gabe and Saphy looked up to see the tall, elegant naiad Atalanta. She stood in the doorway, dressed in flowing white, an arrow drawn on her bow, the last from her now empty quiver, looking for all the world like one of the classical statues where they had first met in the Louvre.

"Leave now, you two," she said in a commanding tone, "Leave. Escape. There is no further help for our sister but for what I can give."

Gabe stumbled over to Saphy and pulled her out of the way, staggering out of the room just as Atalanta unleashed her final arrow which flew across the room with speed and grace, passing right through her sister naiad as she lay in pain and horror on the table, killing her in an instant.

Before Gerard could comprehend what had happened, Atalanta had turned and swept out of the door, her fleet feet carrying her to the exit far quicker than Gabe and Saphy.

Nevertheless, in moments the two of them burst through the double doors and out into the hot Turkish sun. There was no sign of Atalanta or Phobus and Deimus and none of any living Hospitallers, although two guards were slumped either side of the door, arrows through their chests.

Beginning to hear the sounds of panic and footsteps inside the Hospitaller building, Gabe grabbed Saphy's hand and they ran as best they could, her in biker boots, him still barefooted, through the streets of the town, ran until they were completely lost, so lost none of the Hospitallers could have followed them this way.

They were free. Free and in possession of directions to the end of their quest, the real Fountain the naiads had guarded so long.

"I can see why they stopped calling it Mountain of the Goddess and started calling it Goose Mountain," Saphy sneered as they bumped along an increasingly rough road.

Saphy and Gabe had had some trouble making their way out of Bodrum. They had no money, no credit cards, one of them was dressed in essentially a piece of sacking and without shoes. Saphy understood Ancient Greek and Latin but she had little knowledge of modern Turkish, which made negotiating difficult.

Finally, through a combination of mangled Greek and gesturing, they had managed to hitch a lift north to Izmir. Four hours later, having managed to snatch a little sleep, they had had to find someone to take them onwards to Edremit, another four hours. In the end, this had taken the best part of the day and, in Edremit, it had been nearly impossible to find somebody to take them the final part of the journey to the mountain. It seemed, as far as they could gather through the language barrier, that very few people made the journey from city to mountain.

After a long search that took them into the following morning, Saphy had managed to find the one person who was driving to Kazdagi. It was a small truck that looked as if it had been first bought in the 1970s and had been little worked on since. It had an open back that was used to transport chickens, ducks and, the mountain's namesake, geese. With no room up in the cab, both Gabe and Saphy were stuck sitting amongst crates of smelly birds, making angry clucking and honking at the confined space they were trapped in.

While the roads around Edremit had been reasonable to travel on, by the time they got out of urban areas and into the more sparsely populated countryside around the mountain, the roads had become rougher, barely more than dust and gravel, and the suspension of the truck was not so good at dealing with it. For over an hour, the truck bounced up and down on the track, throwing Saphy and Gabe about, slamming them against crates of squawking birds.

A crate of geese slammed across from one side to the other, showering Saphy in feathers and bird stink. The sun beat down and both already felt hot and sweaty even without the discomfort of the journey.

"I mean, I doubt this was how Venus used to travel," Saphy was saying.

"Let's just focus on the end," Gabe said, every part of his body aching from hours of uncomfortable travel, "We're so close now."

"And what will we find when we get there?" Saphy looked uncomfortable and not at all happy, "Is there going to be an army of naiads protecting it? How are we going to handle them, when we saw what just one can do back in Bodrum?"

"That was odd though, why did Atalanta use her only arrow on the other naiad?" Gabe said in response, "Why kill her and not Gerard?" "A couple of reasons that I can think of," Saphy looked pleased to be distracted from the uncomfortable travelling arrangements by the conversation, "For one, they care above anything about their secret not getting out, so killing the naiad in captivity would make sure there was no way of her ever being broken enough to tell."

"That seems pretty harsh."

"That kind of harshness is probably how they've kept the secret for so long. But, there's another reason as well. For the naiads, their virginity, like with Diana their goddess, is an integral part of their existence, it's what defines them. Once that had been violated then she would no longer be a naiad. There'd be no place for her. Atalanta probably killed her out of mercy as much as anything else."

Their debate was interrupted as the bumping of the truck slowed and stopped and Gabe and Saphy were released from the back. Pointing at the truck driver's map gave them a reasonable sense that they might be where they wanted to be. Mostly, they were just pleased finally to stretch their legs and leave the ducks and geese behind. Gabe was not quite sure how he would manage a long walk the way his legs were feeling, but right now it was preferable to more sitting in a cramped, hot space.

The driver pointed them in a direction that he indicated through arm waving sign language would bring them to a river, hopped back in his cab and drove off along the rough, bumpy road. Gabe and Saphy set off into the shelter of the trees, seeking out the sound of running water they could just about hear in the otherwise perfectly peaceful landscape.

The mountain was fairly high but the ascent was not steep. In the distance, they could see the peak of the mountain looking harsh and lacking in vegetation. Behind them they could just about see the sparkling blue of the Mediterranean. Around them, however, was a surprising amount of lush green plants and trees.

The surroundings were pleasant but progress was slow. Both were hot and tired and, without shoes, Gabe struggled to walk on some of the surfaces beneath them. He felt the hot stones under his feet cutting into him, sweat ran down his back and across his forehead into his eyes, but a sense of excitement pushed him on, made him ignore the discomfort for the hoped for goals ahead.

After a while, the road was left far behind and the sun partly blocked out by the shelter of pine trees. Although they knew roughly the right direction to be heading and could still just about hear the sound of running water, neither was entirely sure that they were on completely the right track.

"We're sure this is the right way, aren't we?" Gabe asked, not sure at all himself.

"No," Saphy admitted, "Not really, but we can only hope and keep searching."

"But that could take -- "

Gabe had no chance to finish this thought, however, as he felt Saphy grab his arm tightly and fiercely. She looked suddenly alert as she placed her finger to her lips to keep him silent. A moment later, he knew why as he heard the sound of a snapping branch.

Very gently and quietly they crept up towards where the sound had come from and looked out through the treeline to see a group gathered in a clearing, a group that looked painfully familiar. All were dressed in the black robes and white crosses of the Hospitallers. From one of the hooded figures came the voice of Raymond Gerard, the Grand Prior.

"Consult the map," he was saying, "We must be close."

Another of the hooded figures pulled out and unfolded a large sheet of paper that seemed to show the same contours and landscapes as the one in Gabe's underwater photograph.

"Map?" Gabe whispered to Saphy, "How did they get a map? And then get here so soon?"

"Shhh," was all she responded.

That was enough, however, to alert somebody of their presence. A second cracking sound and Saphy spun round. Not quick enough, though, to prevent two Hospitaller guards from grabbing her. Gabe looked around in panic, but he was free for barely any longer. Another guard clamped Gabe's arms against his sides and the two of them were dragged out into the clearing.

"Ah, I had been wondering when you two would show up," Gerard exclaimed, removing his hood to look straight at them with a triumphant sneer, "There were many times since we first met when you should have left all this well alone, when I would have been happy to have you killed. And, yet, I suppose it is fitting to have you here now, at the end, to have your final moments bearing witness to my new world order."

He laughed triumphantly as Saphy and Gabe struggled half heartedly and unsuccessfully against their captors. There was indeed a sort of inevitability that they would come up against Gerard and his religious fanatics at least once more on their journey. It had been almost too easy to get away from them in Bodrum. It seemed to Gabe, from his life behind cameras and in front of TV screens that their escape had been an unsatisfactory resolution to the adventure.

"You must have had a rather slow journey to only now have come to this point," Gerard went on.

It dawned on Gabe then that it was not a case of the Hospitallers making it up to Mount Ida with surprising speed, more that Saphy and his days of hitchhiking had not been the quickest route up the mountain.

"But how..." he stammered, "How did you know where to go?"

"You told me. You two gave me all the information I needed back at the Castle," he said, still looking smugly triumphant as his guards held Gabe and Saphy tightly in place, "You were the ones that realised the pool beneath the castle held a map. All we needed to do then was go back and copy it."

"But if you knew where to find the map what did you need that naiad for?" Gabe demanded, "You needn't have done those horrible things to her."

"No," he grinned in a way that appeared intended to provoke an angry reaction, "Perhaps not," he paused to let that thought sink in, "But then she could teach us so much more than you two. She had access to valuable knowledge where all the pair of you do is stumble upon things. She could have provided a much more precise location than this map of yours. And she could have revealed, once we reach the Fountain, quite how it must work. Without the knowledge of the Fountain's power all this has been worthless."

"You mean, you never knew how it works?" Gabe asked, surprised, "Or even if it does."

"Of course not," Saphy was, to Gabe's ongoing surprise, the one to answer this one, "That was clear from the naiad's interrogation."

"Indeed," Gerard agreed, happy to let Saphy reveal just how much she knew.

"Professor Robert White knew though, didn't he?" she was the one with a smug look on her face now, appearing keen to show off all her knowledge now that they may not have long to live, "That was what you wanted from him and what he found out tracking all those Hermaphroditus statues around the world. He had all your answers and all you had to do was use your best interrogation tricks to get them out of him."

"But, I don't understand," Gabe, not for the first time, felt his mind was having to race to catch up with Saphy's deductions, "How could you know that Robert White had discovered all about the fountain? How could you know what happened to him?"

"Haven't you figured it out?" she responded, "It was so obvious and yet I couldn't quite believe it. Couldn't believe it because it meant believing too much else that I wasn't ready to accept."

"It's not obvious to me."

"We know just what happened to Professor White," Saphy explained, "We know because we were there. We saw him die. It was Professor White who died at the naiad's arrow in front of the Rokeby Venus. He was the victim in the London National Gallery murder. It was his death that set us both on the path that lead us here!"

"Wait," Gabe, confused, demanded clarification, "You're saying that Robert White, the eminent academic expert in classical mythology, the author of Love's Children; and the transgender woman shot with an arrow at the National Gallery, the one who left the symbol on the wall, are the same person?!"

"Don't sound so surprised," Gerard, the Hospitaller Grand Prior grinned evilly, "It has always been really rather obvious."

"As I said, I had suspected it from the first," Saphy replied, "But something held me back from committing to the idea. Because, to make sense, the theory relies on one important detail."

"The victim was transgender, she looked nothing like the picture of White in his book?" Gabe asked.

"Exactly. In order for us to believe that the Rokeby Venus victim was Robert White, we couldn't believe that he had had himself surgically or hormonally transformed. There was a far deeper physical difference. The victim was naturally intersex, a hermaphrodite. To believe it was Robert White is to believe, truly believe I mean, that a power exists to transform a male body into a hermaphrodite, to believe in a real Fountain of Salmacis."

"But, if it requires such a leap of faith from you then why do you believe Robert White was that woman?"

"Because it's the only explanation that fits...'Whatever remains, however improbable, must be the truth'," Saphy responded, quoting Sherlock Holmes' famous words, "We already know that the victim was killed by naiads, the white feathered arrow tells us that. As I told you before, that's a fairly unique murder weapon. So, why do the naiads kill?"

"To protect their secret," Gabe responded instantly, beginning to follow Saphy's train of thought.

"Right. That means that they must have thought that this transwoman was in possession of some knowledge that threatened that secret, that could lead to the

Fountain of Salmacis. We also know that the victim's clothing was another unusual detail. She was dressed in a plain white smock and no shoes running through the London streets. It meant nothing to us at the time, but it might do now."

"It's what I'm wearing," Gabe realised how obvious a lot of this should have been to him.

"So, she must have recently been held prisoner by these thugs. The victim was never identified because they had a completely new physical identity," Saphy went on, "But that doesn't mean she had no identifying marks. She left a symbol behind, remember, the joined Venus and Mars symbol, right in front of the Rokeby Venus. We were both there, we saw the hurried panic, saw how she headed straight for that particular painting and left that symbol with some painful determination. Whoever she was, she must have known the secret of the painting, what it really depicts and left that symbol as a clue, a warning about the men hunting her, the assassins Phobus and Deimus. Who else knew how to interpret all of that?"

"Professor Cavendish?" Gabe recalled.

"Exactly. So, the victim, the person who left those clues, would have to have a similar background, similar knowledge, maybe even left the clues for Jane herself. It suggests somebody who was a colleague of hers. Somebody like Robert White," she paused for a moment, looking around at the Hospitallers and Gerard, all were staring at her, listening in rapt attention to her laying the whole case out, "Do you remember in White and Gerard's office, you found a piece of paper?"

"Yes, the list of museums: 'Louvre, Villa Borghese, Palazzo Massimo Alle Terme, Uffizi, Prado, Met'," Gabe remembered, "All the places with a Hermaphroditus sculpture. It's what lead us to the Louvre and then to Bodrum."

"So, that is how you managed to make such quick progress," Gerard cut in, "By stealing from my office!"

"You said it listed all the places with a sculpture," Saphy responded to Gabe, ignoring the Grand Prior, "But it's not quite all. An ivory miniature of the Borghese Hermaphroditus was brought back from Rome in the 17th century by the diarist John Evelyn. I looked it up when we were in Paris, suspecting that there had been something torn from the bottom of that list. However, with what we discovered at the Louvre, the missing sculpture never seemed important. At least, not until Bodrum, where we saw Dr. Gerard there baptise his minion from a miniature ivory sculpture that looked very much like the one Evelyn brought back from Rome."

"But that didn't do anything," Gabe added, "We saw it."

"Yes, but that may just be that these guys don't know the secret," Saphy smirked tauntingly at the sinister hooded figures standing around them, "They don't know what White knew, what the naiads knew. There must be some way of activating the waters, of making them transformative, otherwise the secret would have been known years ago."

"So, how could White have known it?" Gabe asked.

"White was a historian, right? A researcher with an interest in rare books," Saphy explained, "John Evelyn's diaries aren't so well known these days as Samuel Pepys', but they have always been read and published. White would have been familiar with them. He would also have known that all the earlier years, the time when Evelyn would have acquired the Hermaphroditus sculpture were compiled much later by notes he took at the time. There has always been an idea that there may be some original lost diaries of those years. What if those diaries from the time he acquired the sculpture contained some other discoveries, some lost information? Evelyn's tomb was broken into in 1992, nobody knows why, but his skull was stolen. Perhaps he was buried with something else as well."

"You're saying that a secret diary or set of instructions for the sculpture and the Fountain's waters might have been taken from his tomb?" Gabe asked.

"And then White, on taking an interest in Evelyn and the sculpture, managed to track them down, managed it and tried Evelyn's instructions on himself. It worked and he was transformed into a new intersex body. Knowing Gerard was interested in his search, he revealed the transformation to Gerard but refused to give up the secret," Saphy speculated, "Eventually, this must have made Gerard angry and desperate enough to use his eunuch assassins to capture and interrogate him. White must have known that his escape would only be a temporary reprieve and so rushed to leave a message that could only be understood by those in the know. He just managed to leave his message for Jane Cavendish before the naiads got him, preserving their secret just a little longer."

"Once again, I appear to have underestimated you, Miss Cross," Gerard had a patronising sneer on his face, "You have done a most excellent job of deduction, but I do not see this realisation being of any more use to you than it is for me. Robert White's knowledge died with him, just as your own knowledge will, very shortly I can assure you, die with you."

"I don't get it," Gabe purposefully ignored Gerard's reference to their impending doom, focusing on straightening out every detail of Saphy's story, "If we always knew the naiads had killed Robert White, then why are you not angrier with them than you are with these guys?"

"Because I understand just why they had to do it," Saphy explained, "I understand why this is a secret that can't get out, why protecting it from what the likes of this so-called monastic order and their wannabe world domination would do with it is important. You, however," she went on, turning her attention aggressively toward Gerard, "Not only would you commit the worst atrocities with this secret if you discovered it, you've already committed senseless violent murder. Jane Cavendish was a good, innocent woman, a woman who did nothing but help people and who did nothing to get in your way. You should pay dearly for her murder. You should suffer for it. I wish every single bit of pain you gave to her was revisited doubly on you!"

As she got angrier and angrier, her face becoming as red as her hair, Saphy struggled against the grip of the two men holding her back. Both men were a good head taller than Saphy but she was fuelled by righteous anger. She tore her way out of their arms and leapt across the clearing, racing toward where Gerard's smug smirk turned to an expression of surprise.

She slapped him violently across the face, scratching her sharp fingernails as they trailed after her hand, causing red stripes to appear across the Grand Prior's face. Her second hand swung after to land a heavy punch into his jaw, while the scratching nails of her right hand grabbed and tugged at his thinning hair.

Her assault was ferociously violent but ended as quickly as it begun. The two large hooded Hospitallers from whom she had broken free took a moment to recover from their surprise, but then they were right back on her, grabbing her arms even as she scratched and tore at their leader. As they pulled Saphy off him, a clump of his hair came away with her hand.

As the Hospitaller guards held her back with an even greater firmness, Saphy appeared confrontational but pleased with herself. Gerard's composure, however, had completely gone, no longer the suave intellectual completely in control of his, and everyone else's, destiny, he looked flushed and flustered. His face was scratched up and deformed by an angry grimace.

"That's enough," he let out a high pitched scream, "Kill them! Kill them both! We will not let them live another moment."

Gabe felt his heart beating faster, even while standing still he felt his breath coming in sort bursts. Just a few minutes earlier he had been feeling the respite of Gerard's decision to keep them alive at least long enough to witness his triumph. Now, after encountering Saphy's rage, the Grand Prior capriciously decided their time was up and Gabe began to feel, with a newfound certainty, that this would truly be it for him.

Time appeared almost to stand still, it was as if Gabe was watching his own life in slow motion as Gerard screamed and shouted and Saphy kicked and struggled. His whole existence of constantly observing from behind his camera left him completely unprepared for being the centre of attention, he just stood stock still.

As he watched, aghast, Gabe saw the tall, sinister shapes of the assassins Phobus and Deimus emerge from the trees and stride across the clearing towards them. Still seeing as if slowed down, Gabe watched as each drew their long ugly curved daggers, the same that had killed Jane Cavendish.

"You have sinned and now will be punished," hissed one in their chilling high pitched whisper.

"We will bring you to the world of dread and fear," the other agreed.

They continued forward as the Hospitallers fell away from them, even they appeared afraid of the fanatical assassins and their implacable progress. Gabe winced as he watched them raise their daggers in unison.

"At last," Gerard screeched at them, "Where have you been? Kill these interfering meddlers right now!"

Gabe shut his eyes as the knife came down and a blood curdling scream split the air.

CHAPTER 4

And then, a moment later, opened them, surprised at the lack of the expected impact. Before him he saw Raymond Gerard, his scratched face distorted in pain. It was him that had let out the scream and Gabe could see why. Rather than turn on him and Saphy, Phobus and Deimus had brought their daggers down slicing into their employer, cutting and gouging into his flesh, causing blood to come spurting and flowing from him. There was nothing efficient about their actions, they were not trying to kill him instantly, rather they hacked and slashed, causing Gerard as much violent pain as they possibly could.

"Did you think you could commit such sinful acts before us and there would be no price to pay?" hissed one.

"You hired us to destroy the wrong and unnatural, so that is what we do now," the other said, slicing his dagger through Gerard's throat until he finally dropped dead at their feet.

Gabe breathed a sigh of relief at the narrow escape from what he had felt sure was the end of their quest. His moment of escape was brief, however, as, with Gerard dispatched, the two assassins turned toward him and Saphy a nasty glint in their eyes. They towered over both Gabe and the guard still holding him back.

Looking up into the bright blue sky, he saw the long arm of one of the twin assassins raise high above his head, the dagger blade glinting in the hot Turkish sun, the blood of their last victim still sticking to its tip.

"And now," the assassin said, "To finish the job. There will be no escape this time."

Gabe felt his knees go weak. He felt as if he was about to faint as Phobus, or possibly Deimus, the twin assassins remaining indistinguishable, raised his bloody dagger to strike. The Grand Prior of Villeneuve, Dr. Raymond Gerard, lay dead at their feet, and Gabe was about to join him.

As the assassin brought down the knife, Gabe flashed back to the events of the past week, witnessing the horrific murder at the National Gallery, meeting with the confrontational and aggressive Saphy, his dreams of fountains and goddesses, the help Jane Cavendish had given and her brutal death, fleeing the police to Paris and then following the clues to Turkey, capture and escape from the Hospitallers, and, more than anything else, the way that Saphy had gradually opened up to him, revealed her scarred and damaged heart and let him in.

He looked across at her, struggling defiantly in the face of death, and all he could think, as the knife slashed down, was about the feel of her soft lips on his, how right and good it had felt kissing her.

The knife, however, never reached its destination. Just as it swung towards Gabe, an arrow whistled through the air, passing smoothly straight through the assassin's hand and sticking squarely in the eye of the hooded guard holding Gabe. Another moment and another arrow struck the second assassin square in his shoulder blade just as he too was about to swing his dagger. And then everything was chaos.

As the arrow struck his hand, the assassin standing over Gabe dropped his dagger, while the guard holding Gabe slumped to the ground, clutching at his face where the arrow had embedded itself. The other assassin swung at Saphy as the arrow hit his shoulder, causing him to swing wide of his mark. The white feathered arrow still protruding from his shoulder, he swung around to see Atalanta at the head of around thirty naiads, all with arrows drawn on their bows.

As soon as they saw this, the group of hooded Hospitallers gathered around their fallen leaders and pulled guns from their robes. The air was filled with the sounds and flashes of gunfire. A naiad and then another dropped to the floor. More of them swung and spun agilely away from the Hospitallers' fire and unleashed a volley of their own arrows, sticking the hooded guards like pin cushions.

Meanwhile, the two bald assassins turned their attention from Gabe and Saphy to the rest of the crowd, obviously perceiving them as more of a threat. Even though one had an injured hand, the other a shoulder, and they were only armed with daggers where the others had guns and bows, they still managed to glide through the crowd, slicing and cutting with their daggers in just the right place to incapacitate both naiads and Hospitallers.

A naiad leapt toward Saphy, but the guard that had been holding her until a moment earlier hit the naiad square in the chest with a gunshot at point blank range, dropping her instantly to the floor. Saphy wasted no time in wriggling free of her captors and grabbing the bow and a handful of arrows from the naiad's quiver.

The guard was back on her in a moment, but in that time Saphy had put an arrow to her bowstring and drawn it back. As the guard made to grab her once more, Saphy released the arrow. She may have not known much of what she was doing, but at that close range there was nowhere the shaft could go but right into her attacker's chest.

The other guard made a lunge for Gabe but Saphy, growing in confidence, had another arrow on her string. This time, at a slightly greater range, the shot flew just off her target, but did enough to pierce the flesh of the warrior monk's arm, causing him to drop his handgun, which Gabe gingerly picked up.

Unable in that instant of panic to figure out how to take the safety catch from the gun, Gabe swung the weight of it into the guard's face, pistol whipping him until he fell into the grass.

Gabe and Saphy now stood back to back on the edge of the clearing, him with a gun, her with a bow with one final arrow drawn on the string, ready to take on anyone just like the rest of the people in that clearing, ready to defend themselves together, to fight for each other's lives not just their own.

Across the clearing, the Hospitallers' superior weaponry was making little difference against the naiad's speed and skill as more and more black robed monks found their bodies ripped open by the arrows of the women in white. While some naiads had fallen, in a few minutes the battle was over and there remained nothing but a heap of black robed fanatics, dead just like their leader, never to discover the secret they had fought for.

Phobus and Deimus now turned back to Gabe and Saphy. Bloodied and full of wounds from gunshots and arrows, they staggered forward, daggers dripping with the deaths of both sides. Gabe and Saphy were ready for them now, however, pointing both bow and gun right at them.

"You want us?" said Saphy.

"Then come and get us," Gabe finished her thought.

The two angry assassins looked around, seeing their victims' armed defiance did not stop them, but the fact that they were now surrounded by killers every bit as capable as them, the beautiful archers with arrows trained right at them, their determination wavered.

"This is not the last time you will feel fear," said one.

"Nor the last sense of dread," said the other.

"We will always be with you," hissed the first.

"You will never sleep easy while we watch," concluded the second as they staggered from the clearing.

The naiads did not follow them. Instead they turned their attention to removing the bodies from the clearing, both their own fallen and their enemies, covering their tracks so nobody could come this far after them.

Atalanta, tall, beautiful, elegant, the dark curls of her hair hardly dislodged by the frenetic battle in which Gabe had seen her personally skewer at least four

Hospitallers with volleys of arrows, turned to the only two other survivors, Saphy and Gabe.

"You're not scared of them?" Gabe asked, referring to the assassins that the naiads had been happy to turn their backs on.

"Naiads are pure, we live by our own strict moral code, those two have no power over us," Atalanta explained.

"And that moral code is what brought you to kill Robert White in London," Gabe went on, "I get it now. And why you had to kill Gerard and his secret society now."

"Indeed," Atalanta concurred, "Keeping the secret of Salmacis' shame has always been more important to us than all else."

"So, then it follows that you haven't been rescuing us here, you've been building up to killing us too, just as you threatened in Paris," Gabe said, "Because you must know that we will not stop until we too find the Fountain and know its secret. I understand that now, and I'm ready for it."

He had never realised he could be so defiant and, as he looked over at Saphy for support, he almost thought he could see a look of pride on her face beneath the piercings and flame red hair.

"Perhaps," if possible, Atalanta had begun to look almost wistful, "And then again, perhaps not. We have never allowed anybody who came seeking the Fountain to find it or to return to the world with their knowledge. Never. And yet you two are different from all those who came before you. We have been watching you throughout your journey and your behaviour is not like the other seekers. You do not seek fame, fortune, death or power, you seek love and new life. You are compassionate. Your attempts to save our sister in Bodrum, while misguided, have taught us that you both have good hearts. Thus, we are prepared to make you a deal that we have never done before and may never again."

"Don't say that you'll spare us if we turn away and leave now," Saphy said, "We've come this far and we'll never leave without finding what we came for."

"No, I can see that you won't," Atalanta agreed, "Our offer is, in fact, just the opposite. We will allow you passage to the Fountain, indeed I myself will even lead you there, reveal the location to you, but there is a condition. You must never return home, never return to your old lives, never speak of what you have seen or done here. The rest of the world must assume you dead or disappeared or we have no agreement. The naiads will find a place for you and will watch and protect you, but if you ever leave do not think that we will hesitate to kill you."

"And if we refuse this deal?" Saphy asked.

"Then we will kill you right here and now instead," was Atalanta's firm response.

They turned to each other, both hoping the other's thoughts were in tune with theirs. They had known each other for barely a few days, albeit some very intense days, and here they were being asked to give up everything back home, to never go back there, and pass the rest of their days with each other. That was a pretty big step to take, especially given a lot of those days that they had known each other had been spent bickering.

"It's not like I've got a lot to go back to," Saphy admitted, "A broken hearted university drop-out. Jane was one of the few people I had a connection to back in Britain, but she's gone too."

"And I'm still wanted for her murder," Gabe added, "That could prove pretty sticky if we ever made it back."

"Yeah, if..." Saphy agreed, thinking, "You know, we've been threatened with death so many times in the last few days, I'm kind of inclined to go with the choice where we don't die!"

"Does that mean...?" Gabe trailed off, excited by the possibilities.

"Yes," Saphy said, decisively, turning to Atalanta, "We accept. Show us the way to the Fountain and we'll happily stay in the sunny Mediterranean and never go back to bloody cold wet Britain!"

And, just like that, in a conversation in which, Gabe felt, more was communicated without words and lasted barely a few seconds, Gabe and Saphy severed all ties with their past lives and took a step forward into a new future together.

They dropped their gun and bow, feeling no more need to be armed. Atalanta, for her part, strapped her bow to her back and returned the arrows to the quiver. Dismissing her companions, she led the two of them on alone.

Quietly contemplating the outcomes of their decision, both now walked behind Atalanta, not really bothering to take in the route that she was showing them. Now that the choice had been made, the quest nearly over, neither quite knew how to put into words exactly what they were feeling and so both remained silent, their eyes on the ground.

Gabe was a little surprised therefore, to find Saphy's hand seek out his, she squeezed his hand and held onto it in a manner that was completely uncharacteristic but proved deeply comforting to him.

The harsh stony ground beneath Gabe's feet began to give way to a softer grass as they pushed through the tree line and out into the baking sun. Gabe felt a weight seem to lift from his shoulders as his sore, aching feet walked on the soft surface. The sound of running, tumbling water had grown louder and louder. Something felt just right, somehow familiar.

He looked up and around him and, sure enough, it was just as it had been in his recurring dreams. Sure, some of the details were not precisely the same, but then the dream had always changed with new details anyway. Never the less, it was hard to say that this clearing with its soft green grass, white flowers and bright, hot sunshine, was not what he had dreamed of.

Just like in the dream, he felt himself powerfully drawn to the running water, the sound of a fountain cascading and splashing. He longed to feel the waters against his skin just like he had imagined so many times in his deepest sleep.

His pace quickened, overtaking Atalanta, as he hurried forward toward the sound of the Fountain, walking now alongside the flowing waters of the crystal clear brook. He had no more need of the supposed water spirit now he knew just where he was going. Even Saphy could no longer keep up as his hand slipped from hers.

And then there it was, looking not so much like his dreams, but in his heart he knew it anyway; the Fountain of Salmacis. It was not the walled stone construction he had pictured, rather a part of the natural flow of the river. It was a waterfall that tumbled over the stones from above, splashing down into the clear waters below, creating an inviting deep pool.

Gabe looked into the pool's water and, sure enough, it was so bright and clear that his reflection shone back at him, just like the Mirror of Venus. It was not a very pretty sight, he was scarred and bloody from the fight, dressed in just a shapeless white smock, the same kind Robert White was wearing when he died. Still, Gabe smiled at last to see that reflection for real in these real blessed waters.

Another reflection appeared behind him, a beautiful face with golden hair. Just like in his dream, Gabe felt the presence of the immortal love goddess.

"Now, your time has come," she said in her soft voice that caused Gabe's body to tingle, "We have arrived."

Shaking his head to rid his mind of the dream state, Gabe saw that the second reflection, the beautiful face beside his, was really that of the dark haired Atalanta, the light of the sun glinting on the water making her hair appear to shine blonde.

"What did you say?" he asked.

"We have arrived," Atalanta said again, "I have brought you here as promised and I will leave you here, but know that we will be here to watch and protect you and your knowledge."

As Atalanta disappeared, Gabe could hold himself back no longer. Not even bothering to strip from his dirty white single garment of clothing, just watching his own reflection, he dived head first into the pool, heading straight for the waterfall's raining fountain.

The moment he hit the water, he was struck by the cold of it compared with the heat of the sun above. Yet this was nothing like the slimy sludge of the water in the pool beneath Bodrum Castle. Every moment in this pool made Gabe feel more refreshed and relaxed, he let the water wash over every fibre of his being, cleansing him of all the horrible things he had seen and all the pains of his body over the past few days.

Finally, he broke the surface, letting the water drip off him. It felt good to be so cool, wet and clean. He basked in the joy of it for a moment, but there was something missing. Just as in his dreams, there was something not quite there, something unsatisfying, leaving a bitter edge to the cooling pleasure of the Fountain.

He looked into his reflection, down at his body. Sure enough, there was no change. Whatever magic could be in the Fountain, it had done nothing for him. He was still looking at the same old awkward, introverted Gabriel Herrison. He had not been touched by the beauty of Venus at all.

Gabe had never known that he would be so upset to find, at the end of everything, that nothing had changed and nothing would, that this whole adventure would leave him the same Gabe as had begun it.

There was a splash and Gabe's reflection shattered in concentric ripples. Moments later, the flame red hair of Saphy broke the surface. Gabe looked around to see her massive biker boots kicked off on the river's grassy shore. Otherwise, like Gabe, she appeared to have dived in fully clothed, her torn and pinned t-shirt was becoming wet and see through, her mini skirt fluttering in the river's current.

She swam the few languid strokes over to him and smiled, a warm, reassuring smile that stopped the tears that had begun to well in Gabe's eyes.

"Didn't work then?" she said, "I was so sure it would, so sure at last that I could believe in it."

"Serves us right, I suppose," Gabe replied, "For getting caught up in such a fantastical story. I guess it really was a wasted journey."

"Not wasted," Saphy said, "This journey hasn't ever been just about the damn Fountain, it's meant more than that. More to me, anyway."

And then, as the waters of the falling Fountain cascaded around them, Saphy put her arms around Gabe, pressing his body into hers. Her lips sought his and they began to kiss, a long, lingering kiss that went on and on as the river's current swirled around them. Gabe let the waters of the fountain wash over him as other emotions and sensations crashed around his body. It was just like all those dreams, the waters of Salmacis washing his body and the soft touch of a beautiful woman bringing that body to life, every touch causing an electric tingling sensation to run right through him, causing blood to rush to his head, not to mention between his thighs.

Only now, looking at the woman before him, he did not see the unattainable, barely imaginable image of the love goddess with her perfect features and flowing blonde hair. Now he saw something that thrilled him even more, the very real, yet still beautiful, sight of a girl with flame red hair, piercings in her eyebrows, nose and tongue and a body covered in tattoos, the girl he realised that he had come to think about, feel about and fantasise about more than ever could an image of a goddess.

Saphy was what he cared about, not Venus, not Hermaphroditus, not Salmacis, or any of those mythological distractions. None of them were touching him, kissing him, thrilling him in the way that she was right now beneath the raining waters of the Fountain. Every slightest touch that she gave him, brushing through the water was a new thrill, her hands in his wet hair, her breasts pushed against him through their soaked clothes, her lips kissing his, her tongue stud inside his mouth.

She pulled at his wet white tunic, the single item of clothing he wore, tugging it over his head and casting it into the fast flowing current that took the river away from the waterfall. Gabe watched his clothing float away, followed quickly by Saphy's miniskirt, before she planted a series of soft kisses on his lips.

"But," gasped Gabe, "I thought...You were pretty clear you were a lesbian... "

"Yeah, well, we're only here because deep down you always wanted a woman's body," she said, dismissively, "So, I guess that's good enough," she laughed, "Come on, what are you waiting for?"

With that encouragement, Gabe reached out and tore off Saphy's ripped and pinned together t-shirt, putting his fingers in one of the existent tears and ripping the whole thing in two to expose Saphy's body, painted in tattoos, dressed in just her underwear in the cold clear waters of the river.

They kissed and kissed again, their wet, near naked bodies, pressed against each other, tangling around each other. Gabe's lips felt a shiver run through them with each kiss. They felt alive, growing and changing. It was almost as if Saphy's kisses had given him a set of fuller, more sensitive lips to feel every touch of her own.

As they kissed, Gabe fumbled with Saphy's bra, still feeling a little awkward and self-conscious. Her hand, however, found his and, in a moment, her pale white breasts were on show beneath the shining sun. Gabe cupped her breasts in his hands running his finger around her hard nipples as Saphy pushed him back through the tumbling fountain of the waterfall so that his back was pressed against the wet rocks behind.

She slipped her last remaining piece of clothing, her panties, over her legs and let them drift away with the current, before wrapping her legs over where Gabe's were pressed against the rocks. She pulled him into another kiss, running her hands through his hair and pushing her breasts against his chest. Every part of his body that she touched was now shivering and tingling just like his lips.

Beneath the water line, Gabe felt his manhood stiff and hard, ready for what he eagerly anticipated was about to come. Saphy's hands ran down from Gabe's hair, over his shoulders and across his chest. Between his legs she held his hardness while her other hand slid between her own thighs.

Soon Gabe felt Saphy guiding him between her legs, into her wet spot, her body gliding against his as his hardness slid inside her. Saphy's moist pussy felt tight as it clasped around his erection, holding him in a way he had never been held before. He had never even been anywhere near this close with a girl before and now here was Saphy rubbing up close to him, riding down over him. It was all that Gabe could do not to release completely the moment he felt himself inside her.

At first Saphy simply began to grind her groin into his, letting him grow more accustomed to the feel of being inside her. Gabe had to remind himself that all this was just as new to her, given her previous proclivities. He could only imagine that this was the first time his aggressively lesbian companion had allowed herself to be penetrated by a man. Yet she was the one to take control here, Gabe only too happy to be lead. Soon Saphy began to pick up a rhythm to push herself further against him and back, riding his manhood as the waterfall tumbled around them.

As Saphy's thighs pressed against his, her legs wrapped around him, pulling him deeper inside her, Gabe could feel a tingling in his skin and the muscles beneath as if every fibre of his body was growing and changing. Looking beneath the water line, Gabe could see their legs tangled together, a mass of winding pale naked limbs, almost hard to tell which were his and which hers. The ugly tattoo on Saphy's thigh listing slurs and insults and its "sticks and stones" motto was all that showed where was Saphy's leg and where Gabe's. But, for a moment, it almost appeared as though this image was repeated across both of their thighs. Then, a second later, it seemed to have disappeared completely, both sets of legs appeared smooth and unblemished.

On top of this, Gabe noticed something else as he pushed his hips up to meet Saphy, burying his hardness deeper within her. It may have been a trick of the light, refraction from the cold, clear water, but it almost looked as if those hips had grown wider, and his waist was narrower. Under the waterline his body seemed to match Saphy's in its shapeliness. It appeared to Gabe as though his flat skinny body had curves, feminine curves. But he was probably imagining things.

Saphy tossed her head back as she started to pull Gabe deeper into her, her muscles constricting tighter around his hard aroused parts. He looked at her with awed desire, her flame red shock of hair, pierced face and naked breasts looked so good to him in the shower of Salmacis' fountain. The water fell over Saphy's fiery hair and ran down her shoulders. Gabe's eyes widened in surprise to see the Chinese characters, stubbornness and free will, indelibly marked into Saphy's arm begin to fade. It was as if the tattoos were written in nothing more than marker pen ink and the fast running waterfall was rubbing them clean off. It had not been an optical illusion. Saphy's tattoos really were being cleansed from her body.

Saphy's body was not, however, the only one that was shifting and changing under the fountain's free falling water. Gabe pushed his chest out as the curve of Saphy's breasts arched away from him, his nipples starting to feel tender and every time Saphy brushed across them he felt more excited than ever. As Saphy noticed this, she started to fondle his chest and he was shocked to notice small bumps around his nipples that had never been there, while they themselves stuck out as hard as his erect manhood.

Saphy raised her eyebrows at the sight of what appeared to be pubescent breasts emerging from Gabe's chest, but did not stop. She laughed and wrapped herself tighter around him, pushing her own bosom against his chest. Gabe could no longer deny that changes were happening in his body, that it was not illusion or imagination. With Saphy's breasts pressed into his, soon he had a chest that nearly perfectly matched her, a complete pair of grown, adult mounds of feminine flesh.

Always somebody who found the feminine form much more desirable than the masculine, Saphy barely hesitated as Gabe's body feminised in the fountain. If anything it seemed to drive her on, her interest in Gabe's mind and soul now matched by a desire for his body. If Gabe had thought it felt good before, now was something else. Their feminine curves pressed together as Saphy drove his penis deeper and deeper inside her, writhing and grinding with gleeful neediness.

"Oh my God," Gabe heard a sigh come from his mouth in a voice that was his and yet not his. A voice that was as transformed and womanly as his body was becoming.

"I think 'my Goddess' would be more appropriate in the moment," Saphy grinned.

As she said this, Gabe watched her open mouth, the stud glinting on her tongue. He could see Saphy's lips open in ecstasy and could tell that she was as perfectly in this moment as him. As their bodies entwined and moved in a single rhythm, her wrapped around him, him inside her, their skin and muscle shifting and changing to reflect one another, it was as if they were one united creature, one body working towards achieving its ultimate pleasure.

Saphy gasped as the water splashed around her and the muscles between her legs tightened around Gabe. Her breathing was fast and heavy, her body shook. Gabe knew that she was reaching her climax, knew that, penetrated for the first time, her body could take no more and was releasing wave after wave of pleasure just in the way the waterfall flooded over her. As Saphy came Gabe glanced at her chest and saw the ugly scar there begin to fade and the tattoo heart beneath it to wash away.

Light headed, new body parts still being explored, Gabe remained pushed as deep as he could be inside Saphy's wetness. In her moment of passion, however, Saphy's hand pulled him further against her, straying and exploring parts that he was not yet even aware of. Sliding beneath where their sex parts united them like the original Hermaphroditus and Salmacis, Saphy's questing fingers found something new and began to stroke it.

Gabe nearly lost his mind at the feel of Saphy fingering his labia. For all the transformation his body had been through he had not realised this most female of parts had opened between his legs. As Saphy slid two fingers right into his newly emerged and aroused pussy it all became too much for Gabe. He could hold back no longer. Thrusting himself against her, he felt his orgasm sweep through him, ejaculating his love deep within her as the fountain's waters swept everything else away.

Afterwards, admiring the shape of his new body in the clear mirror of the lake, Gabe could still hardly believe it. He had breasts, a narrow waist, wide hips and smooth shapely thighs. His face had changed. It was still sort of him, sort of recognisable, but it was her. It was him as he would be if he had been born a girl. It was the face that he had always subconsciously wished for but never truly understood. His long hair was still wet with the waterfall, but he saw there was a streak of colour it never had before, a bright flame red seemingly taken straight from Saphy's head.

He turned to her and smiled, noticing her examining and admiring his body. Hers had changed too. Where he had a streak of red running through the fringe of his hair, hers had a streak of his dark hair in its place. Where once her body was covered in rainbow stripes, Chinese letters and Greek poetry, now it was bare, a clean slate. All except for the symbol on her arm, the circle and cross, the female symbol, the mirror of Venus.

He reached to point this out to her and she instead caressed his opposite arm. Looking at himself, Gabe now noticed another thing that had never been there before. A tattoo had appeared on his own arm, the mirror of Saphy's, but for one thing, the circle and cross had an arrow too. It was the combined symbol of male and female, Mars and Venus, that had first begun this strange, unpredictable quest.

Gabe remained amazed as he absent mindedly fondled his new curves. Only his penis and balls remained to show his remaining masculinity. He had truly become a hermaphrodite just as the legend told.

"It actually worked," he finally articulated, "It really does turn men like Hermaphroditus."

"I wasn't sure, but I thought this was the secret," Saphy responded, "What the Hospitallers never understood."

"That it needed a woman's touch," Gabe laughed, it all becoming clear to him, "The transformation into a woman needed the physical love of a woman to happen."

"That's what Professor White knew all along," Saphy agreed, "It's not just the fountain, it's sex too that does it."

Turning back to his own mirror, the waters of Salmacis, Gabe admired the twin reflected images of himself and Saphy, reflected in the water, but also their bodies reflecting each other. This is what it had all been for. For a moment he thought he saw a third figure, a tall, statuesque blonde familiar from all his dreams and fantasies. She looked straight at him, smiled in a proud fashion and then faded from time and memory like Saphy's tattoos.

The green slopes of Mount Ida drop down toward the warm blue waters of the Aegean Sea. With the bright Turkish sunshine and clear blue sky behind it, the heights of the mountain stand clear central to the view from across the narrow Mytilini Strait. Here the clear Aegean waters wash against the white sands of a beautiful Greek island. This is Lesbos, the island once home to the famed poet Sappho and her devoted female disciples. Such is the impact of the poet's words and thoughts that the island has long since leant its name to any 'of the Sapphic persuasion' in giving them the epithet of 'lesbian'. Since such a time the island has become something of a pilgrimage site-cum-holiday spot for same sex female couples.

At this point in the garden of a small, pretty villa perched on a clifftop above the Mytilini waters one of Sappho's modern followers lay sunbathing naked beside her latest companion, her new lover. College dropout

Persephone Cross' usually pale skin had tanned a golden brown colour, while her hair had grown out to hang around her shoulders, now coloured blue apart from a streak of undyeable brown above her forehead, the piercings in her nose and eyebrow glinted in the warm sunlight. She was more relaxed and contented than she had been in a long time and that was reflected in the clean slate that was her uninked, unblemished skin, save for the single tattoo on her arm. This tattoo was a near match for the similar one reflected on the opposite arm, the one belonging to the equally curvy female form sunning herself beside her.

Ms. Cross' partner, sometime photographer Gabrielle Herrison similarly soaked up the day's warmth, her matching pair of firm, naked breasts similarly tanned by the endless Greek summer. Her whole body, in fact, was a sort of mirror of her lover's. From the similar tattoo on the opposite arm to her cascades of dark wavy hair, a single red streak in the spot where her lover's was dark. The only great difference lay between her legs where Ms. Herrison's little penis and balls nestled between smooth feminine thighs, the only enduring reminder of a masculine past she had been only too happy to sever her ties with.

Life on Lesbos was easy and pleasant for the wealthy English lesbian and her hermaphroditic lover. There were sunny days, sandy beaches and warm seas. They enjoyed healthy delicious Greek food and plenty of wine and were well known to many of the island's all girl night spots. This had been what neither could have expected the day both decided to visit London's National Gallery on a grey, wet English morning, but then life can take some strange turns even without ancient secret societies and mythical curses.

Propping herself up on one shoulder, the newly feminised hermaphrodite turned to face her lover, her reclining body unconsciously adopting a posture reminiscent of many artistic renderings of classical reclining nudes, but one that was off special significance to the two of them. Her gaze took in all of her lover's naked body, still finding it hard to believe that she could look at her like this, let her gaze linger on those naked breasts and not be met with a scornful look or withering comeback.

"Do you ever miss it, Saphy?" she asked, "Your old life, I mean, England, Cambridge all that."

"Just Jane Cavendish," Saphy replied wistfully, "Her getting mixed up in this is the only thing I regret, but it's not something I can go back to. There's nothing else for me back there." She paused and her moody expression lightened into a fond smile, "Besides, Gabby" she went on, "I wouldn't give up any of this for anything."

Her hand gestured to show "any of this" took in the sunny skies, the sea beneath the cliff, the villa and Gabby stretched out beside her. Gabby smiled back and leaned in for a soft, slow lover's kiss.

"I've been thinking of a new tattoo," Saphy said, "New ink for my new life."

"What sort of thing?" asked Gabby.

"I wonder how much it would cost to get the Rokeby Venus."

They both laughed and kissed once more as Saphy reached over to caress the symbol magically inked into Gabby's arm, the circle with its cross and arrow that had first brought them together.

"And how are you liking yours?" she asked, her one hand still on the magically transformed ink while the other strayed between Gabby's legs.

"Oh, so good," Gabby replied, although whether in response to Saphy's question about the tattoo or the fact that Saphy's questing fingers had slipped beneath Gabby's masculine genitalia to stroke along the wet labia that now existed beneath was unclear.

This amorous moment was, however, quickly interrupted by the sound of a splash below the cliff on which they lay. A piece of stone had obviously crumbled from the cliff top and tumbled the long drop into where the surf smashed against the rocks below. Both Saphy and Gabby glanced across at the source of the sound and then spun all their attention towards it, open mouthed in shock and fear.

Matching looks of panic crossed both of their faces because the sight they saw emerge above the cliffs like a horrible mirage was one they had thought never to see again. First came bald heads and aggressive, determined scowling faces, then tall, imposing bodies and long, strong arms. Finally the deadly twin assassins Phobus and Deimus stood over them, their great, looming figures casting long shadows as they seemed to block out the sun itself. Even though they had obviously just climbed the sheer surface of the cliff and were dressed in long dark robes, neither seemed to have broken a sweat.

Gabby felt a surge of nausea welling up in her stomach and her breathing quicken to a point where she was almost hyperventilating. Lying naked in the open air she felt so exposed. Just moments earlier she had felt utterly carefree, her masculine parts were still stiffened from Saphy's stimulation of her feminine parts and now her mind was thrown into a wild panic. She suddenly felt very awkward in her new body, like it would not obey her. She was rooted to the spot. There was nowhere to run to, nowhere to hide, no way to fight back.

Looking across at Saphy, Gabby could see that she felt just as exposed and helpless. Saphy's eyes were darting around this way and that, desperately searching for a solution, for some hope of escape, and finding none. Just like Gabby, Saphy knew that, surprised, naked and on the floor, there was little they could do against the vicious, fearful killers that had manifested themselves before them.

"You did not think you could forever evade fear and dread," hissed one in his high pitched lisp.

"We have searched for you, avoided the powers of your keepers and we have come for you now, unholy abomination," the other responded.

One now stood right over Gabby and the other in the same position above Saphy, just as paralysed by fear. Each drew their wicked looking sacrificial knives and raised them above their heads so that they glinted in the sun. A look of triumphant nastiness played across both faces.

Gabby glanced across at Saphy. Taking Saphy's hand in hers, she closed her eyes and waited for the inevitable, waited for the final conclusion of their adventure. As she did so Gabby realised that she no longer felt scared or sad or alone. She felt fulfilled. After years of feeling like an outsider, of feeling awkward, like there was something missing or something not quite right, finally she had become somebody he was happy with. The story that had held such fascination for her as a small boy was now her own story. She had discovered a part of her that felt like her true self and had found someone to share that self with, someone who also now felt like a part of her. Everything that had happened to her recently had fulfilled everything she ever needed, even things she did not know she needed and, as Saphy had said, she wouldn't trade it for anything. She knew that even if she had to die she would have no regrets. She would die contented at last.

Thinking all this Gabby waited for the blade to fall, for her life to be savagely ended just when it had started to matter, but nothing happened. She opened her eyes to see the same figure standing over her. Something had changed though, the hand that had been holding the knife had dropped it and now, in its place, a white feathered arrow stuck through the flesh, it's razor sharp head projecting from the other side.

A moment after Gabby opened her eyes a second arrow sung through the air, striking the assassin in the chest and making him stagger backwards. As he stood, stunned, on the cliff top it was clear that he had not at all expected this, the element of surprise was turned against him. A third white feathered arrow struck him square in the forehead and he tumbled over the cliff edge. After a second's deathly silence a sound, half splash, half splat, signalled the assassin's end on the rocks below.

There was still the second man, however, advancing on Saphy with his knife raised. As Gabby opened her eyes, though, and the second arrow hit the first assassin, she noticed his companion's attention falter for a moment, not sure whether to persist with his own single mindedness or to assist his accomplice. Despite her position naked and vulnerable on the floor, Gabby seized this opportunity to take advantage of the assassin's momentary hesitation. Swinging her bare leg round, she hit him across the back of his calf just as he brought the knife down at Saphy, causing him to trip backwards and his swing to miss by an inch.

"Get away from her, you fucking freak," Gabby shouted angrily, seeming to rouse Saphy to action at the same time.

"Wow," said Saphy, impressed, "You really have taken on a little of me."

Saphy grabbed the other knife that the first assassin had dropped when the arrow had shot through his hand and stabbed it with all her might into the second assassin's thigh just as he recovered from Gabby's trip. The assassin stumbled backwards and the two naked young lovers sprung to their feet. As the assassin, blood leaking from the wound in his leg, staggered back to a standing position and began, now with some effort, to raise his knife once more, Gabby swung her right fist and connected violently with his jaw. As he spun round, before he could reorientate himself, Saphy landed a matching blow on the opposite side of his head.

Stumbling backwards, the assassin now stood right on the edge of the cliff top, balanced precariously and unable easily to keep steady with the knife wound in his thigh. At that point one further white feathered arrow sung through the air. It passed through the assassin's windpipe barely hindered and flew straight out the other side. A look of confusion crossed his face as blood bubbled up through the hole in his neck. Then, like his companion before him, he tumbled backwards, falling from the high cliff down to the rough waters below. And that was the end of the feared and dreadful assassins

Phobus and Deimus, simply vulnerable mortal men after all.

Gabby and Saphy turned to look for the source of the arrows that had so ruthlessly dispatched their assailants. Sure enough from out of the tree line around the edge of the pleasant villa stepped Atalanta the naiad. Dressed, as ever, in her flowing white dress, a quiver full of arrows strapped to her back and a bow in her hand, she looked completely composed as if nothing unexpected had happened. She looked over the naked lovers but her expression displayed no great emotion. Then, for a moment, she gave them a smile, or the closest they ever saw to a smile from her.

"Don't forget," the naiad said, "We're always watching."

With that she disappeared without giving either the chance to respond. Gabby did not know quite whether to feel safer or uncomfortable with the idea that all they did on Lesbos would be watched by the naiads, but in that moment she was just glad to be alive. She felt a rush, a thrill that her life had been threatened once more and she had come through unscathed. If anything she felt more alive than ever. Looking across at Saphy, Gabby could tell that the same thought was on her mind.

"Now, where were we?" Saphy said, kissing Gabby on the lips, allowing her studded tongue to invade Gabby's mouth, pulling her into an embrace and pushing the naked mounds of their breasts together.

"But, they're watching," Gabby nervously indicated where the naiad had emerged from.

"So?" said Saphy as she fondled Gabby's breast, "Let's give them something to watch then."

Her kisses moved down from the soft lips of Gabby's mouth, over the curves of her body, to the other lips between her legs. Gabby felt weak at the knees as Saphy moved beneath her male parts to lick at her wetness. As her feminine sex became aroused, Gabby felt Saphy's hand on her manhood. Saphy began to stroke it, getting it stiffer and stiffer while still eating out her other parts at the same time. Gabby was in hermaphrodite heaven, experiencing arousal as a man and a woman all at once.

Her knees trembled and buckled, no longer able to support herself with all the pleasure Saphy was bringing to her. Gabby collapsed to the ground. Lying there naked, her erect penis sticking out from her feminine body, Gabby looked to see her lesbian lover leaning over her. Saphy opened her legs and straddled where Gabby lay, impaling herself on Gabby's hardness until their bodies were united once more.

As she looked down over the curve of her breasts to see Saphy, her once combative companion, now writhing her naked body above her, Gabby no longer cared who could be watching. She admired the way Saphy's breasts rose and fell as her breathing grew heavier and reached over to hold those warm orbs, stroking and fondling her. She was completely exposed, they both were, with nothing to hide behind any more. This was how their lives would be from now.

As Gabby reached the exquisite moment of her double climax, she could only think of how happy she was. Happy to be alive. Happy to be here, here with Saphy.

THE END